SHATTERPROOF

XEN SANDERS

RIPTIDE
PUBLISHING

Riptide Publishing
PO Box 1537
Burnsville, NC 28714
www.riptidepublishing.com

Shatterproof

Cover art: L.C. Chase, lcchase.com/design.htm
Editor: Sarah Lyons
Layout: L.C. Chase, lcchase.com/design.htm

ISBN: 978-1-62649-460-2

First edition
September, 2016

Also available in ebook:
ISBN: 978-1-62649-459-6

SHATTERPROOF

XEN SANDERS

RIPTIDE
PUBLISHING

TRIGGER WARNING

This story contains content dealing heavily and sometimes graphically with the subjects of suicide, self-harm, depression, and obsession.

If reading any of these topics is triggering to you, please stop. Walk away. While it's important for me to depict stories of mental health and surviving suicide, particularly in underrepresented Black and non-Black POC communities, it's more important to me that you take care of yourself.

Be good to yourselves, always.

—X

TABLE OF CONTENTS

1

"My name is Saint," he said, "and I kill everyone I love."

Saint stared down at the digital recorder in his palm. Seconds ticked by on the screen. His black-polished fingernail underscored the blocky numbers, accusing with every moment he stared, silent in the sluggish, slow heat of the balmy Georgia night. He was supposed to be telling his story. Recording the things he knew, so he could piece together the things he didn't.

This was pointless.

He lifted the device to his lips again, hesitated, exhaled. "I call myself Saint, but I . . . I don't know my real name. I don't know where I came from. As far as I can tell, I'm over two hundred years old. I haven't aged a day in that time. But sometimes . . ." He wet his lips. "Sometimes I start to fall apart. Sometimes I grow weak, faint. Until . . ." His heart rolled over, a heavy thing weighted with pain. ". . . until I fall in love. I've loved . . . God, too many. Calen. Michael. Remy. Dorian. Philippe. Arturo. Victor. Jake."

He closed his eyes. Jake. Jake and his grass-green eyes; Jake and the way he'd breathed *Saint, Saint* as if the name was a prayer to save him. It had been eighteen years, and still he remembered the way Jake's hands had spanned his hips, and how those hands had been so emaciated and feeble when his eyes glazed over and his body just . . . *deflated*, like there was nothing inside to hold it up anymore. He'd been the last. Saint *wanted* him to be the last.

He couldn't stand to do this again.

"They always die," he whispered, then pressed his mouth to the recorder, the little stipples over the speaker scraping against his lips. "It's always the creative types. Artists. Musicians. Painters. Authors. Poets. They're brilliant. They're beautiful. They're the only ones who can make me *feel*. Everyone else is monochrome, but for me they're all the colors in the world and even when I want to resist, I can't."

He swallowed, thick and rough. "But then . . . something happens. This fire goes off inside them, and they become . . . *God*, I don't know how to describe it."

He opened his eyes and stared blankly across the room, his dark little warren of odds and ends collected over the decades. Then he looked at his arm, touched his chilled skin, traced his fingers over the patterns marked on his flesh in shimmer-dark ink. Right there— the firebird, brilliant in its sparks, coiling from his wrist to his elbow. That was Jake, burned forever into his skin.

"Transcendent," he said. "Like a phoenix, just before it dies . . . only they never rise again. It's like they're burning apart from the inside out. Like their souls come alight and they're bleeding them out through their art. And I . . . I think it's my fault. I don't know what I am. Some kind of incubus, maybe. I've never met anyone like me. But because of me, they burn out. They die. And for a little while, I don't feel so weak anymore."

He swore softly under his breath. Each word was a noose, tightening around his throat.

"Every time, I hope it will be different. Every time, I . . . I become a murderer all over again. I can't believe it's not because of me. I've been in denial for too long. It's like I'm being punished for loving, but I—I just want to figure out what's causing this." His grip tightened on the recorder; the plastic cut into his palms, the heat of the battery warming his hands through the casing.

"So I can figure out how to stop."

He paused the recording and hit Rewind. The track skipped back to 00:00, then started to play. His own voice lilted out, crackling faintly, racked with things he wished he knew how to stop feeling when every time broke him all over again.

My name is Saint, and I kill everyone I love.

What would happen, he wondered, if he never fell in love again?

He stopped the audio. Erased the track, tap-tap-confirm, yes, absolutely sure. Started again, pressing his mouth to the recorder and feeling its plastic slickness against his lips like a dead, mechanical kiss.

"My name is Saint," he said, "and I can't remember who I am."

He shut the recorder off, pitched it on the table, and walked away.

✳ 2 ✳

Grey wondered who had found him.

He'd thought he planned it better than this. Quiet and alone in his apartment, the pulsing throb of gut-deep, grinding music drowning out any sounds he might make: the noise of the gunshot, his cries, the low quiet whisper of the loa come to take him through Bawon Samedi's gates.

It hadn't been an easy choice, though it had felt increasingly like an inevitable one. As if a road that once branched in many directions had narrowed down to a single path, one walked by many feet before his, one that drew him along step by step until he couldn't have turned back if he wanted to. And he hadn't. Wanted to, that is. No. No, he'd wanted this.

And then he'd fucked it up.

He'd considered more silent methods at first. Something less absolute and terrifying than the rifle in the mouth, angled *just so*, to make sure there'd be nothing left of his brain, the top of his head completely gone. Quieter methods were more likely to fail. He might get one wrist slit the right way and not have the strength to slit the other, waking up later in a pool of his own blood but still *waking up*. His body might force him to vomit up pills. Hanging, both the rope and the chair might slip at the wrong moment. A pistol to the temple could graze, miss, come out the other side.

But the Hemingway solution . . .

Brutal. So beautifully brutal; so very effective. His last work of art, splattered in blood and flesh over a canvas of gleaming floorboards.

That was how it worked, when you really wanted it. You didn't advertise it. You didn't broadcast it to anyone who might stop you. You held it close, a precious little secret clutched to your chest, and planned it out so nothing could go wrong.

Only something had.

He remembered pain, blinding and hot. The wavering disc of the overhead light cut in chop-chop-chop streams by the blades of the ceiling fan, strobing in and out. The wet feeling of blood pooling, and the sad, quiet thought of:

I hadn't wanted to feel this.

I hadn't wanted to feel anything ever again.

Then a scream he didn't recognize, heavy footsteps, the clatter of equipment, the jumble of sirens, his body moved about like a lifeless sack while he felt like he was floating outside it, watching while deft, capable hands took his vitals, staunched the flow of blood, eased something soft under his head. The ambulance jouncing around him. And a pale figure next to him, in an EMT's blues.

He struggled to focus. The lights inside the ambulance were too bright, everything blurring in and out in a haze of white. Strange eyes. Strange eyes like the rose color of sunset just before twilight, as if they wanted to be violet but something inside had bled out crimson to taint their color. Dusk, he thought dimly. They were the color of dusk, flecked with motes of sunlight, set against a white, sullen face framed in a messy thatch of black. A delicate face, grim with a sort of quiet, constant fear that lined his angled eyes and set the line of his jaw *just so*. He didn't look old enough, Grey mused with a sort of detached clarity. He didn't look old enough for those slim pale ghosts of hands to be touching Grey's body, piecing him back together, saving his life.

Stop, he wanted to say, but his tongue was leaden and bloated and filling his mouth. *Don't. Don't bring me back. Just let me go.*

But first, tell me what you're so afraid of.

Those hard, angry dusk eyes flicked to him as if the pale man had heard him. He studied Grey intently, while the siren shrieked a high keening wail and the ambulance careened around a corner hard enough to make everything inside jerk and rattle.

"Why'd you do it?" he asked, so soft Grey almost didn't hear him.

He swallowed thickly, forced his tongue to move. His voice struggled to come up, a cold and unmoving lump in the bottom of his throat. "Does i-it . . . does it matter?"

"Yes." The pale man lowered his eyes. His hands rested on Grey's chest, the wings of white doves, feathers tipped in black. Black-painted nails, chipped and gleaming and throwing back reflections of those pensive, pensive eyes. "It always matters."

You're wrong, he wanted to say, but his voice still wouldn't work. He closed his eyes, fighting past the dull throb of pain to find thought, find reason, find anything other than an overwhelming sense of failure.

But against the backs of his eyelids he saw strange sunset eyes, and felt the warmth of hands resting quiet and sweet just over his heart.

"What . . ." He choked, coughed, his mouth a desert. "W-what's your name?"

A low laugh answered, oddly melodious. "I thought we were talking about questions that mattered."

It matters, Grey thought. *It matters to me.*

But he couldn't get the words out. The dark was coming fast.

And when it swallowed him down he went willingly, and hated that on the other side waited a blinding and damning light that shone too bright to let him hide from anything.

Even himself.

✳ 3 ✳

Saint looked down at the man on the stretcher as his pale, coyote-gold eyes sank closed. Thick, dark lashes swept to the high planes of ebonwood cheeks. Blood smeared down the side of his face, leaking from the bandaged wound that had carved a furrow in his scalp and even now spread crimson on the gauze, the bright red of an arterial bleed. Blood loss left an ashen undertone beneath dark skin, blood loss and strain—but Saint thought he would be all right.

He wondered why the unconscious man had done it. So often he wondered why, when so many of his late-night calls were suicides. Suicides or drunks, and in both cases usually by the time he arrived, there was nothing he could do. Every once in a while, though, he found one like this. One who'd done it wrong, or changed his mind, or gained some grace or curse of divine intervention.

What would this man call it if he were awake?

A blessing, or a curse?

His driver's license, fished from his back pocket, said *Grey Jean-Marcelin*. Thirty-seven. Even in his license photo he had a sort of melancholy beauty, cut in the articulated hollows of his cheekbones and the precise, full shapes of his lips and the stark angles of his eyes. His name sounded familiar, but Saint couldn't remember where he'd heard it. He tended to dip in and out of the pulse of Savannah every twenty years or so, going to ground until anyone who might remember him—who might remember that his face hadn't changed in decades and the people he dated tended to end up shriveled, desiccated echoes of themselves, sealed away in body bags—had moved on.

At least there'd be no body bag for this one. Not tonight. He'd have an impressive scar, cutting a channel down the tight, close-cropped burr of his prematurely white hair, but he'd live.

"Hey," Nuo said from across the stretcher. "Xav."

It took a moment for his alias to sink in. He was still getting used to being Xav, and not Saint or Dominic or Ambrose or any of the other names he'd used over the years. This time, he was Xav Cascia. The name had made him laugh when he'd come up with it, printing it onto a fake ID and laminating it with a little machine that made false identities easier than ever in an age when verifiable information was harder and harder to lie about. St. Frances Xavier Cabrini and St. Rita of Cascia. He always took his fake names from Catholic patron saints, and this time he'd chosen the patron saints of impossible causes.

Nuo snapped her fingers in front of his face. "*Xav.* You okay?"

He shook himself, tearing his eyes from Grey's unconscious face, and looked up into the lines of exhaustion etched under the creases of his partner's dark brown eyes, her pointed chin nearly disappearing into the high collar of her oversize EMT uniform. "Why wouldn't I be?"

"You always get mopey over the suicide squad."

He scowled and carefully slid another folded towel under Grey's head to elevate his skull. There wasn't much more he could do for him other than bandaging and compression, now that he was sure Grey wouldn't bleed out. He was just the ferryman, fording the river between life and death over and over again. In a few minutes, Grey would be the ER nurses' problem. Stitch him up, bring in the shrinks for a psych eval, make sure he was safe to go home under his own recognizance. After tonight Saint would never have to see him again; would never know the answer to that burning question of *why.*

"I just don't get it," he murmured, and dabbed a trickle of blood from Grey's cheek. "I don't get why people wouldn't do anything and everything they can to live."

"You can't know what's going on in his life." She leaned over to check his pulse. "Whether it's personal or chemical, people have their reasons. Maybe he lost someone. Maybe he couldn't get over a failure. Or maybe he's just another artist who glorifies it as dramatic and poetic, and doesn't quite get that it's real."

Saint stilled, a feeling popping in his chest like globules of bursting sickness, knuckles curled against Grey's cheek. He was so cool, as if already dead, and his stubble had the texture of volcanic stone against Saint's skin. Every sensation was more real than real, a heightened awareness deeper even than the adrenaline rush of that critical moment between life and death. It prickled on his skin—a whisper, a promise unfulfilled and only waiting for him to speak the other half of a terrible vow.

"Artist?" he choked out.

"You haven't seen the flyers around the Market?" She snorted. "God, you need to get out more. They call him 'the Grey.' There's a Gandalf joke in there somewhere, but he's a painter. Got an installation down at the Savannah Gallery. Really dark, gritty stuff. Haunting. You'd probably like it."

"Yeah," he said, his lips numb. He stared at Grey, really *seeing* him, the vividness of him, and his tongue dried to the roof of his mouth; dread recognition wrapped barbed-wire coils around his heart. "Yeah, I probably would."

$$ \ast\mathfrak{E} \quad 4 \quad \mathfrak{Z}\ast $$

Bon dieu, he hated answering questions.

Grey picked at the cold, congealed lump of hospital Jell-O, but the tinny flavor of artificial strawberry couldn't wipe away the sour aftertaste of the questions the psychiatrist had asked him, or the bitter taste of defeat. His hands shook, blood loss making his fingers clumsy and numb—and the morphine residuals weren't helping, though the nurse had shut off the drip hours ago. He wouldn't be holding a brush again for a while.

For a while.

Did that mean, then, he was back to thinking in terms of days, weeks, months, years . . . instead of in terms of minutes?

That was what the psychiatrist had asked him. If he could think about tomorrow. If he could *see* tomorrow, instead of just an empty nothing cut short by a line of red.

What kind of question is that? he'd demanded.

The only kind of question there is, the psychiatrist had answered. *The only one that matters. Think about tomorrow, Grey. Think about what tomorrow could be for.*

The only thing tomorrow is for is getting out of here.

We'll see, Grey. We'll see.

He wondered how long they'd keep him here, feeding him Jell-O the same color as the blood he'd spilled all over his floor. How long they even *could* keep him here legally, when at this very moment a nurse or orderly or shrink was likely watching his every move and reading some arcane symbolism into how clumsy his fingers were on the spoon. Some message he didn't know he was giving off, that said instead of going home he'd be on his way to Memorial Health in the back of a padded truck.

He closed his eyes. *I'm not crazy. That's the worst part.*

It was just the sanest choice I could have made.

The door creaked open, the hinges squeaking. Grey lifted his head, opening his eyes, and set the unappetizing Jell-O cup down. A short, slim man stepped into the room. He moved like someone who made an art of not being seen, Grey thought. Someone who didn't like to be noticed. He pictured the man hiding in the brush with the dapples of leaf-light falling over his fey, fragile features, and wondered why he looked so familiar.

The EMT.

Recognition clicked. The EMT from last night. Those soft dove-hands on his chest, a throatily accented voice that sounded Irish and yet was just *off* enough that he couldn't place it, dusk eyes that burned with a question he didn't know how to answer—almost accusatory against the backdrop of sulky, petulant beauty that seemed too young for someone old enough to pull him back from the banks of the Acheron.

He'd almost thought he'd imagined him. Some fever dream of blood loss and despair.

Yet even now he felt the echo of his touch, handprints branded on his chest in phantom warmth.

The man pulled out a chair from beneath the window, slipped out of his jacket, tossed it over the table, and sank into the seat. Dark art played down his bare arms in rolling lines, chasing each other through flowing tangles of black ink and singing against his skin like musical notations. Grey caught himself lingering on the tattoos, on the faint shimmer of them—as if the ink had been drawn in silver and shadow. But when he lifted his gaze . . .

The man was watching him, steady and intent. Waiting.

As if he wanted something.

Grey frowned. "Are you just going to sit there and stare at me?"

The man shrugged one shoulder and folded his arms over his chest, slouching down in the chair, slender frame sprawled with artless grace. "You're not supposed to be alone."

"I'm not?"

"They say the first few hours after a suicide attempt are the most crucial." That soft accent lilted, beguiled, husky and strangely knowing. "Or the first few hours after you wake, at least. You were out for quite a while."

Cold realization sank in Grey's gut. "You're here to make sure I don't try it again."

"Unless you have someone you'd like me to call."

He flinched. That cold, sinking feeling froze into a solid block of ice. "No." *Not anymore. Who would . . . I don't . . .* "There's no one."

"Then you're stuck with me."

"I didn't know suicide watch was in an EMT's job description."

"I'm on break."

He narrowed his eyes. "That's not the real reason you're here."

"Ah," the man said, both brows rising, that lyrical accent rolling and sweet. "He's a clever one, he is."

"What do you want?"

Another of those shrugs. Insouciant, taunting, as taunting as the peak of slim brows and the steady, pinning stare of half-lidded eyes. "Maybe I'd still like to know why. Why the renowned painter Grey Jean-Marcelin wanted to take his own life."

"I didn't tell the headshrinker. What makes you think I'd tell you?"

"Because I'm not going to judge."

"That's what they all say."

No answer but silence. Searching, expectant, wanting an answer he couldn't stand to say, waiting for him to turn his gaze inward and see the things he'd blinded himself to for so long. The air felt too thick to swallow, and he dragged in a struggling breath, looking away, looking for anything but a weighted gaze that just wanted a simple answer.

He landed on the jacket, and the name tag clipped to the breast pocket. "Xav?"

The man smirked, a pretty thing of pouting, full lips that seemed made for sighing breaths. "That's one thing they call me."

"Implying it's not your real name."

"Why would I need a fake one?"

"You tell me."

Xav—or the man calling himself Xav—tilted his head to one side; his wild mess of hair drifted across his face, a few inky black strands curling their tips against his parted lips. "An answer for an answer."

Grey clenched his jaw. "Is this a game to you?"

"No," Xav said softly. "I need to know why you want to die."

"Shouldn't you be asking if *want* has become *wanted*?"

Xav parted his lips, then stopped. Something flickered in his eyes, something doubting and soft and hurt. Something that Grey thought might just be the first hint of the real person underneath this coyly mocking facade, the same person who had glared at him so angrily in the ambulance last night, as if what he'd done to himself had personally hurt the other man.

"I think I'm afraid to know," Xav said.

"Why?"

"Because if you want to do it . . ." He exhaled heavily. "I can help you."

"How?" Grey demanded, but Xav only avoided his eyes, looking blankly at curtains turned luminous by the glow of afternoon light. "*How?*"

"You want to find out?" Xav stood, picked up his jacket, and slung it over his shoulder. Sparking eyes fixed on Grey again, still so sharp, so accusing. "Stay alive long enough to get out of here."

Then he turned and walked out, leaving Grey with more questions than answers . . . and no idea what to think.

The door banged closed. The last Grey saw of him was a toss of dark hair. Then he was gone, while the silence of the room resonated with the one thing Grey couldn't stand to ask himself:

How badly do you want to die?

✳ 5 ✳

Still wet from his shower, Saint curled up in his papasan chair, burrowed into his nest of blankets, and wondered why he'd done it.

Offering like that. He'd sensed Grey's attraction; the man looked at him like he was all colors and symmetry, itching through Grey's fingertips and waiting to be bled onto canvas. He knew that look. He knew what it would lead to. And he'd thought about it for the rest of his shift, through the walk home, through a shower that could never quite scrub off the medicinal smell of the ambulance. He'd gone in there like some kind of knowing seducer, offering Grey not his body but a ticket out the door Grey had already kicked open for himself.

Wrong. Sick. Stupid. *Dangerous.* He wasn't just playing with fire. He was playing with his own *life*, teasing at a mortal man who hadn't a clue what he'd stumbled into, hinting he could help him die. All it would take was one wrong word to turn too many eyes his way and transform his quiet, secret unlife into a public spectacle.

Murderer, the headlines would say. *Vampire. Incubus. Monster. Freak.*

Hiding among us in plain sight, and using love to kill.

He felt like a sick vulture, hovering and circling while death came by slow inches.

Did that make what he'd done any better? Just because Grey Jean-Marcelin wanted to die, that made it perfectly acceptable to prey on the man's life to save his own?

Biting his lip, he traced a fingertip over the tattoo coiled on his left wrist. A gecko in blocky Aztec patterns, thick geometric lines. Arturo, tail looping onto the back of his hand. What shape would Grey take? A coyote, to match those tawny eyes?

Those eyes. There was so much desperation in them, but the light behind them wasn't dead yet. Even pallid and covered in his own blood, Grey had been beautiful: full of a fire waiting to be stoked—smoldering embers that could, if ignited, send him up in the most brilliant flames of passion. There was a heart inside him starving for touch, almost as hungry as Saint's own. He could *feel* it, that *click* waiting to happen, a rightness that said they could fit together in a gestalt greater than they were apart.

And in dying, Grey would become immortal.

God, Saint was really thinking about this, wasn't he? He'd never done it on purpose before. Not openly, not consciously, even if it had always been in the back of his mind with the others. A wall of denial making him think this time it wouldn't happen again. This time that rush was just the first vibrant bloom of new love, and not the sickness inside him. This time it would be all right. This time he wouldn't end up alone again. This time he could *keep* someone, or at the very least let them go safely. He'd hoped he could find a way around it, hoped it would *stop* if he recognized the signs and left, but he'd never said, *Here, now, is someone who can answer my need.*

A life thrown away willingly isn't really taken, is it?

He stared down at his shaking fingers. His veins made blue branches in the troughs between his knuckles, marking the valleys of his tendons. Valleys that sank a little deeper than they had just a few days ago, that pulled a little harder, until it made a quiet, deep ache shoot up the bones of his arm when he did something as simple as clench his fist. It was starting already. He'd tried to wait. Tried to hold out. Eighteen years. Eighteen years of pretending he was normal, of burying his guilt, of trying to forget the quiet acceptance in Jake's eyes as he'd faded away.

He tilted his head back against the edge of the chair and watched the sky lighten outside the window of his little tower home, the sun reaching up over the city to swallow the stars and the night into its hungry burning mouth. Shivering, he wrapped himself tighter in the blankets' protective cocoon and pressed the recorder to his lips, and thought of that soft, full, deeply rich mouth asking, *"Does i-it . . . does it matter?"*

It mattered.

It mattered more than anything.

"I don't want to kill him," he whispered. "But god . . . I don't want to die."

✳❧ 6 ❧✳

Grey waited over a week before he finally broke.

They'd kept him in the hospital for four more days. Four more days of IV fluids and tepid Jell-O; four more days of giving the shrink all the right answers to make her think he was sane, safe. He'd made an error in judgment, and his brush with death had scared him back onto the straight and narrow. He wanted to live, he'd told her with just the right choke in his voice. He'd wanted to live the moment that muzzle flash had burst in his face, shocked through him with the terrifying reality of what he was doing. He must have flinched, he'd said. He must have flinched, changing his mind at the last minute, saving his life. He'd lived. Praise the loa, he'd lived.

He'd always hated lying. But in so many ways everything about his life and career was a lie; this really wasn't any different.

So he'd told his lies. He'd slept. He'd recovered. He'd let people poke and prod at him, and endured the pitying looks of the nurses when days passed without a single visitor. Not even the downstairs neighbor, who'd apparently heard the shot and called it in instead of leaving him to bleed out.

Who would come for me? he'd thought, staring at the ceiling bitterly. *I climbed so high into my ivory tower that no one could reach. I shut myself away where nothing could hurt.*

He couldn't remember the name, the face, of the last person he'd called *friend*. She was just a ghost of soft brown skin and remembered laughter, and the way she used to shove his shoulder and tell him to snap out of it when he'd start brooding. That had been in the early days, back when it was just *brooding* and not this consuming mire that sucked out . . . everything. Memories. Faces. Names.

Aminata. Her name had been Aminata, with her gentle Wolof accent and the scar on her hand where she'd scraped herself open on a broken two-by-four at the summer construction job where they'd met, in uni.

He couldn't remember how many years it had been since she called. He didn't know if her number was even in his phone anymore, or if she'd pick up if he called. She'd been the one who'd bought him champagne for his first gallery showing, who'd asked him to hold her hand in the moments before her first big interview at that downtown architectural design firm, who'd burned his rejection letters and thrown her own out the window and stood on the edge of night with him to say, *Fuck it. Fuck this world if it don't know us, if it don't need us.*

Until the day she'd said, *You've changed, Grey. You've changed, and I don't know you anymore.*

He'd smiled, thin and bitter. *No one knows me. Everyone knows who I am, but no one knows me.*

Yet Xav had looked at him as if he did. As if he could see right through him, and understand something Grey couldn't quite articulate himself. Each day, he'd hoped to see those strange, dusk-colored eyes. When he'd tried to sleep, he saw them: looking down at him with such fury, snapping and wild. Watching him, lit bright as fire by the sun shafts through the window, as if he could see into the heart of Grey and know everything wrong with him, even as he murmured his name with such red, mocking lips.

Touching him, and tugging at something dark and heavy and needy in the pit of his stomach.

He paced his apartment for the hundredth time in five days since they'd let him out, following a path of wood worn dull, the finish eroded away practically in the shapes of his footsteps. He'd done almost nothing *but* pace. His answering machine blinked, demanding he listen to the voices of his agent, the reporters, everyone asking questions he couldn't deal with, shouting into nothing after he'd let his cell phone die and unplugged the landline's receiver. The veve hanging over the hearth went untouched, the candles and incense unlit. Food tasted like sawdust. His paints looked too dull, the colors gone. He couldn't sleep. He didn't know how to just pick up and start again like it hadn't happened, like he didn't still want it.

He was stuck. In limbo. Purgatory. Reaching for heaven or hell, he didn't know, but he needed someone to grasp his hand and pull him either way.

This was insane. He couldn't be such a goddamned failure that he was thinking about—about turning to some pretty, pale Dr. Kevorkian. About letting someone *kill* him.

But the police had confiscated his shotgun, a condition of not being drawn up on charges for the most ridiculous law on the books, when actually committing the crime of suicide put the criminal beyond reach of prosecution. He'd been put on some *list*. He'd never pass a background check to buy another gun, and he didn't know who to ask about buying one illegally. If he couldn't even manage the most foolproof way to die—though he still couldn't figure out how he'd *missed*—then he'd botch another method too.

He fingered the line of stitches running in a sharp diagonal line from just above his ear to the curve of his skull, worrying at it fretfully. Fucking hell.

He needed help.

You could just . . . live, a voice whispered inside him. A long time ago, that voice had been louder. Stronger. Firmer. Full of hope. It had sounded like Aminata, with her sardonic laughter.

But now, it was so quiet he could hardly hear it at all.

He snagged his keys and headed down to the lot before he could talk himself out of it. His hands shook as he tried to fit the key into the ignition of his truck, and he swore before jamming the key in, flicking the headlights on, and starting the engine. Maybe Xav wouldn't be there. Just because he'd been on graveyard shift when Grey was picked up didn't mean he would be now. Or that Grey would even catch him, if he was out on calls.

Stop. Stop overthinking it and just . . . drive.

So he drove, with the streetlamps leading him on like halos and the trees lining the close-hemmed roads leaning over him as if they were herding him, the long fingers of Spanish moss ushering him on his way. The thick Georgia darkness was a choking blanket smothering him in its heat, oppressive and trying to strangle the life from him. He almost wished it would. Save him from doing this. Whatever *this* was.

I'm falling for some kind of sick joke. I must be.

The lights of the hospital shone bright ahead. To most they were a beacon of hope, safety, promise; to Grey they were the sterile medicinal scent of bland gray walls and the feeling of being trapped, bound in shackles made of someone else's thoughts about his mental health. He stopped on the verge of the curving drop-off lane that looped in front of the emergency room entrance; he kept the engine running, fingers hard against the steering wheel, leather sweat-slick against his palms, foot hovering over the gas. Any second now. Any second now he'd talk himself out of this ridiculous idea, floor it, and drive away from this completely stupid, completely *illegal* situation. There was no way in hell anyone with even remotely trustworthy motives would offer to just . . . help people commit suicide.

Maybe he's as crazy as you are.

Maybe he wasn't even there. A few people loitered outside the sliding glass doors, orderlies and nurses on cigarette breaks, holding their smokes between two fingers with that practiced air of veteran smokers. An ambulance was parked off to one side, out of the way, the back doors open. He couldn't just walk in and ask for Xav, could he? He—

A young woman slipped from the back of the ambulance. Tiny, Chinese, her hair clipped back messily and drifting into her face, a few tendrils catching on the shoulders of her uniform jacket. He remembered her: the other face hovering over him, her fingers on his throat, his pulse, her dark eyes seeming to mark streaking trails on the air in his wavering vision. She settled to sit with her legs dangling over the edge, brushing against the rear fender, and plunked an insulated nylon lunch bag into her lap. A moment later Xav joined her, ducking the low roof of the ambulance and swinging out with lithe grace before slouching next to her with a cellophane bag dangling from his fingers.

Grey's nails dug into the steering wheel. He'd never given a face to Bawon Samedi, the vodou loa of the dead, but right now Samedi was a pretty waif of a man with a jaw as delicate and fine as misted glass. He looked... tired, Grey thought with a sort of surreal, distant numbness. As if something had been sucked out of him since Grey had last seen him, leaving just a little less weight inside the lovely shell holding him together. His lips were paler; reddish-dark shadows circled his eyes, made only starker by the slim dashes of eyeliner framing his lashes.

An unexpected stab of concern, spearing up behind his ribs, forced Grey to tear his gaze away, looking fixedly out into the street. He didn't know that man from Adam or the devil, and considering what he was about to walk into, there was no room for ... whatever this was he was feeling. This *pull*. Either he was going to do this, or he might as well go home and figure out what to do with himself. Figure out if he could live the rest of his life painting empty things with no soul, because the voice that kept whispering *Do it* had cut the soul from him and eaten the pieces.

And figure out if he'd ever find the courage to try again, on his own.

Neg di san fe, his granmé would have said. *Bondye fe san di.*

People talk and don't act. God acts and doesn't talk.

So if he was going to act, he had to act now.

He sucked in his breath as if he could swell out his chest with bravery instead of a strange mixture of terror and anticipation, then killed the engine and stepped from the truck, locking it behind. He felt like a damned zonbi, shuffling awkwardly up the drive with his hands stuffed into his pockets, trying to look casual. He almost turned around and walked away, but that would be even more obvious.

The two were engrossed in conversation over their food. As he drew closer, Grey could make out the label on the bag in Xav's hand: a bag of dried apple crisps. He picked up on the tail end of their conversation, their voices low and close.

"—but is it helping?" the young woman—her name tag said *Nuo*—asked.

Xav shrugged and twirled a crisp between his fingers. "I keep deleting the recordings and starting over again."

"You can't *do* that, stupid." She flicked his arm, and was rewarded with a wan smile that didn't quite reach his eyes. "Seriously, it helps.

My therapist said for amnesia cases, repetition and reinforcement therapy can—" She broke off, Saran-wrapped sandwich halfway to her mouth, as Grey stopped a few feet away. She blinked owlishly up at him. "Sir? Are you lost?" Her eyes widened. "Hey— Wait, you're—"

"You came." Xav's cool, smooth voice stopped her short. Guarded dusk eyes flicked over Grey. "You're looking better."

"I don't feel better."

Nuo took a huge bite of her sandwich, her wide eyes darting between them. "Xav?" she mumbled around swallowing her mouthful, but he only stood, shaking his head.

"It's all right. I'll be back."

He fixed Grey with a shrewd glance, then tossed his head and turned to walk away. Grey glanced over his shoulder, but no one was even looking at them—except for Nuo. Heart beating a furious dance against his lungs, he hunched his shoulders and trailed after Xav, shoving his hands so deep into his pockets, his jeans threatened to drag off his hip bones. He felt like a junkie scoping out a new dealer, and tried to remind himself he wasn't doing anything wrong.

Except he was. Suicide was illegal in every state, assisted suicide another name for first-degree murder, and if Xav didn't get the chair for getting caught, he'd at least end up with life in prison plus a few more years for the theft of whatever medical equipment he used to do it.

Stop overthinking it.

Xav led him around the side of the building, to a shadowed nook just past a doorway marked *Employees Only*—one of many brick insets that made the tall hospital walls look almost corrugated. Xav ducked into the enclosed, boxlike space, while Grey hovered on the sidewalk just outside.

"Get in here," Xav hissed.

"Is there room?"

"There's room."

"But—"

A slim hand snared his shirt and *pulled*. Grey choked on a sound, stumbling forward and bumping his arm against the brick before sidling inside. His shoulders barely fit into the narrow crevice, and he flattened himself against the wall, sucking in his stomach as if that could somehow keep him from touching the pale, pretty man standing so close to him; keep him from feeling the warmth of his body heat filling the small space and washing over him in prickles like licking tongues. He caught a faint scent: soft clean skin and fresh shampoo and something boyish and warm as candied apples. His fingers curled helplessly at his sides, and he fought to ignore the sudden dryness of his mouth, the heat crawling down his throat, the tumbling inside him that felt like something had come unmoored and drifted away to rattle about freely inside his chest.

Xav's sultry little mouth quirked; his eyes glimmered against the deep-cast shadows in the little nook. "Am I making you uncomfortable, Mr. Jean-Marcelin?"

"No, I just…I…" He didn't even dare breathe. One deep inhalation and he'd be pressed against that slender body and wondering just what the fuck he was feeling, when this sudden sparking breathlessness didn't belong to a man who was already dead. "There's just . . . um . . . not a lot of room in here."

"There is not."

"You. Um." Grey licked his lips. "You don't look well."

"I am not well." That quirk widened into a smirk, lazy and feline, as Xav swayed closer. "Are you afraid I'm contagious?"

"No." He shook his head. Bondye, Xav barely came up to his shoulder, yet the man had him cornered like a cat with a mouse, and all Grey could do was freeze and stare, and wonder when that soft, luscious mouth would open on killing teeth. "You . . . you said you could help me."

"Perhaps." Xav tilted his head; dark hair fell across his eyes in a tangled shag. "Tell me something. Are you attracted to me?"

Grey flattened himself hard against the wall. That thing rattling inside his chest crashed into his heart. "*What*?"

"You heard me."

"Okay." He swallowed; there had to be a block of wood lodged in his throat, because nothing was going down and his voice would barely come up. "I've seen some weird pickup acts, but this one takes the cake."

"It's not a pickup. I can't do anything for you if you're not attracted to me. It doesn't work."

"But— I—I—"

Xav's lashes swept downward, their sooty curves distracting, hypnotizing. "You don't like men, then."

"No!" Panic started to needle through him in little darts. "Wait, no, yes. I like both! I mean . . . men and women, I just . . ."

"So you like me?"

"I . . . I mean . . . yeah. You're . . . I just . . ." His fingers twitched. Xav was so *close*, that scent like green apples and burned caramel nearly dizzying him until he couldn't think straight; something wasn't right, his thoughts receding until he had to reach through a fog to find words. "You . . . you get to me. But you also weird me the hell out."

"Fair enough." Xav's laughter sounded like he smelled: tart-sweet, burned about the edges. He leaned back, setting his narrow shoulders against the wall and splaying his fingers against the brickwork. His eyes glittered. "My shift is over at 3 a.m. There's an all-night coffee shop around the corner. The Pot, or something asinine like that. Meet me there."

Grey pressed his fingers to his temples. "I thought you said this wasn't a pickup line."

"It's not. Consider it more of a . . . client assessment."

Xav pushed away from the wall and angled toward the exit from the narrow space. His body brushed Grey's: like being touched by fire caged in glass, smooth and sleek and full of burning grace. Grey closed his eyes and held his breath and tried to pull his head back on right. He didn't . . . *do* this. He never had. He'd always had trouble seeing beauty in people, save for his family. Everywhere he looked, everyone he turned to, he saw people living with these strange, quiet voids inside them, desperately seeking beauty and yet never finding it, their skins nothing but flaking paint over the decaying tangle of human pettiness and selfishness and loneliness and hate and sadness and all that terrible complexity that made being human so *hard*.

So he painted what wasn't there. What he wished would fill those voids, but never could. If only because he hoped that somewhere out there, someone would look at his paintings and see . . . and see . . .

What was missing inside themselves.

What was missing inside Grey, too, when he had a hollowness all his own.

He'd never found that missing *something* in anyone else. Had given up trying, after a few abortive relationships that had ended in tears. Girlfriends, boyfriends, it always ended the same way.

You never even see me. I feel like your job, while you're wedded to that canvas.

Be honest, Grey.

I'm just a placeholder for something you'll always look for, but never find.

And the worst part was that they'd been right. He'd tried to love them. Tried to feel something, anything, over years when it had gotten harder and harder to feel anything at all, everything vanishing under a numbing filter that couldn't do more than accept the inevitability of it when another one left. He just . . . didn't have the energy to care. Didn't have the energy for much of anything at all. So he'd kept it for the one thing that lasted longer than any human love built on the fundamental misunderstandings needed to feel like you could *touch* someone who was worlds and galaxies away, but close enough to tell themselves the same lies.

Yet here was this fey, sly thing, this man who looked barely more than a boy, brushing up against him and filling his head with dizzying things, making his stomach draw taut as a bowstring waiting to snap.

Xav's body heat pulled away. Grey opened his eyes. An eternity had passed for him, a lifetime of memories flashing hard and cutting deep, yet in the second that had split between them, Xav had just brushed past him—only to pause, glancing over his shoulder with something wicked glinting in his eyes.

"Besides," he said, "I think you'll feel safer in a public place."

"Why would I need to feel safe?" Grey asked, but Xav curled a hand against the wall and swung himself lightly around the corner like a child on a playground merry-go-round, slipping out of sight. Grey leaned after him, watching his back as he drifted away. "Xav? What's that supposed to mean?"

Xav only flicked his fingers over his shoulder.

"Three o'clock, Mr. Jean-Marcelin," he said, sweetly accented voice rolling over the night, as sultry as the heat. "The devil's hour. You'll get your answers then."

7

Saint leaned against the side of the ambulance, stole one of Nuo's cigarettes, and turned it over in his fingers without lighting it. The taillights of Grey's truck receded, wavering red eyes lighting the night like watchful, accusatory demons. For just a moment, he thought he caught a flash of golden eyes in the rearview mirror, looking at him with a mixture of desperation, skepticism, and a hope that he couldn't stand. That wasn't a weight he could bear.

But he'd put it on himself, and he'd carry it if Grey wanted him to.

Nuo settled next to him and nudged him with her elbow. "What was that?"

He glanced at her mildly. "What was what?"

"Seriously?" She twisted her lips. "So you're going to pretend like Hottie McDeathwish didn't just drag you off into a dark corner somewhere."

"I dragged him, actually." He idly stroked his thumb down the length of the cigarette, lingering over the tiny difference in texture on that dividing line marking the filter, staring down at the little chip marks in the polish on his thumbnail. He'd lost a flake here intubating an old woman who was choking on her own vomit. A chip there performing CPR. Scraped the entire edge off on the crash cart for a cardiac call. Little bits all chiseled away to save lives, as if that could somehow even out his debt. His lips tightened, and he looked away. "Don't call him that."

"Eh?"

"Deathwish. It's not funny. It's his choice." He closed his eyes. That old feeling was back in his chest, that pressure like something was sitting on his heart. "Let it be his choice."

It has to be his choice.

"Xav . . .?" Nuo asked softly.

He opened his eyes and looked down into her puzzled expression, her brows knotted up, her nose wrinkled. What would she think, he wondered, if she knew who and what he really was? He'd known her for a few years now, but sometimes he didn't understand her. She had her own quietness, her own thoughts, her own things held close to the chest, but she locked the doors of the precious glass safe of her heart with a smile instead of with keys made of razors and tears. Sometimes he thought he knew her. Sometimes he thought he never could. As if what he was made it impossible to see and know a human heart.

Or maybe what he wanted to see wasn't there at all, and he was filling in her silences, her nothings, with what he needed from her.

Was that all he was seeing in Grey? Something he needed, and nothing more?

The CB radio crackled from the front of the ambulance. He turned away, and tucked the unlit cigarette behind his ear.

"Call," he said, and hoisted himself into the passenger's seat.

One more life to save, then, before he found another life to take.

✳꧁ 8 ꧂✳

Grey stared at his watch and told himself for the thousandth time to just walk out of here and go home.

And he couldn't figure out, for life and for Bondye, why he wasn't listening to that voice inside his head.

He'd been waiting in the shop for hours, tucked into a window booth and trying to convince himself he was people-watching, looking for inspiration for one last series of paintings. But as the hours wore on and tired nurses in stained, ill-fitted scrubs faded into post-last-call hipsters in skinny jeans and thick glasses, he had to admit he hadn't come for the coffee. If what he was drinking could even be called coffee. Some kind of sugary half-caf caramel soy . . . Colombian . . . spritz . . . something. It had enough caffeine to make his leg jitter, but it wasn't worth listening to someone half his age talk over the entire café about how it wasn't about the Weeknd's *music*, but about the iconography of his *hair*.

Like these perfectly coifed children could understand Basquiat. Like they understood what it meant to be made of the clay earth of Port-au-Prince, and to mix it with blood to make his paints.

You're being an art snob again, Grey. This is why you're miserable and alone.

He smiled to himself and toyed with his coffee stirrer, glancing out the wide picture window. He wasn't usually out at this time of night. The devil's hour, Xav had called it. The hour when he was often making magic, cutting it out of himself and giving it color and shapes. He couldn't remember the last time he'd just had a cup of coffee in the wee hours of the morning, alone yet surrounded by the murmured solidarity of the other outliers awake when everyone else was asleep in their beds.

In moments like this, when smiles crept across his lips and he caught himself tracing the arc of descent of a falling magnolia leaf, watching for just that right moment that would never exist again, when it floated so perfectly . . .

He almost felt normal. Almost felt like he used to years ago, before he'd become a building trying to stand against an earthquake when his foundations were weak and crumbling.

"Need a top-up?"

He glanced up. The barista hovered over him—a slender older woman, cut from sharp angles, her pale green eyes almost livid against the stark whiteness of her face. Those eyes raked over him, assessing. She'd been eyeing him since he first came in, and with every refill. Like he wasn't supposed to be here.

She was probably right.

He held up his mug. "Still have half. Any more and I'll either have a heart attack or go into a diabetic coma."

"That's one way to die."

Her accent almost reminded him of Xav's, albeit more distantly related—rather how his mother's Haitian Kreyole accent had been a watered-down version of his grandmother's thicker native speech. But when she said *That's one way to die* in tones as dryly lilting and sardonic as the man he was hoping would help to kill him, it struck deep and shivered something cold inside him.

He parted his lips to speak, to ask where that accent was from. But the bell over the door jingled and Xav stepped in, peeling out of his uniform jacket to leave a clinging white shirt stretched over his gamine chest, lazily rumpled around the waist of dark blue uniform pants that slouched low on narrow hips. Grey ignored the pointed fingers digging tight into his chest, watching as Xav scanned the room, gaze searching, before landing on him with a spark of recognition. As he drew closer, though, he cast a veiled look at the barista. The woman tilted her head, studying him through narrowed eyes. A strange glance passed between them before Xav turned away with something that, to Grey, seemed almost like forced diffidence.

"Mr. Jean-Marcelin." Xav smiled thinly and draped his jacket over the back of the booth. He had a cigarette tucked behind his ear, and Grey wondered if he was a smoker. "Thank you for waiting so patiently."

"He's been here a while," the barista said. "I should have known he was waiting for someone like you."

Xav paused, his hand resting on the seat back. His eyes glazed over with a chill, and he looked at the barista again, guarded and silent. But she only smiled, unreadable, strange, and lifted her carafe.

"Get you anything?"

"Plain coffee. Nine sugars," Xav said flatly.

The barista whistled softly under her breath, but pursed her lips and strode away, back toward the counter. Xav's gaze trailed her, his brows knitting, before he shook his head and slid into the seat across from Grey.

Grey frowned. What had that been about?

"Do you know her?" he asked.

"Never seen her before. I don't really come here."

"Then why'd you want to meet here?"

Xav arched a brow. "So I wouldn't be recognized."

"I suppose it's wise not to leave a trail when making a deal with the devil."

A slow, pleased smile spread pink lips. "Is that what you think I am? The devil?"

"I'm starting to wonder." Grey leaned back and traced a fingertip around the rim of his coffee cup. "Before we have this conversation, I want to know your real name."

Xav blinked, blinked again, then glanced over his shoulder. At the door, at the barista, at the college student in lensless glasses and a hand-crocheted orange scarf in the middle of August, then back to Grey. He propped his chin in his hands, lips pursing, then shrugged one flippant shoulder.

"Don't have one."

"Everyone has a name."

"I don't." Such a knowing look, drifting over Grey as if he could see the hard, swift whisper of his heartbeat driving the question. "But I'll answer to Saint. No last name."

Saint. Grey mouthed it, letting himself feel it without sound, without getting the color of his voice all over it. Even if it wasn't a real name, it suited him, he thought. Better than Xav. Saint for a man who looked at him through long lashes with the darkly penetrating glance of a sinner, and called him *Mr. Jean-Marcelin* with the lips of an angel.

"Why Saint?" he asked.

"That's a long story." Xav—*Saint* shrugged again. Those shrugs were starting to irk Grey, as if they were calculated to make *nothing* out of what was very much *something*. "One I don't wholly know the answer to. I only remember my life back to a certain point."

"What point?"

Soft lips parted, closed, compressed. Saint looked away from him, out the picture window. His eyes lidded. No shrug this time. No taunting, sweet-tart dismissal. Just that lilting voice, rolling over cold, heavy words.

"The point when I woke up alone, with no idea who I was."

Grey curled his hands around his coffee mug and soaked in its warmth, and pretended he hadn't—for just a moment—wanted to reach out, to touch one of Saint's pale hands. "Your friend was saying you have amnesia."

"Something like that." Saint sighed. But after a moment his jaw tightened, worked from side to side, before he turned hard eyes back on Grey. "But we didn't come here to talk about me."

"You already know what I want. I just need to know how it works. How do you steal drugs from the hospital without getting caught?"

There. It was out. Blunt as a hammer, and smashing down just as hard. The weight of it would crush him, making it real, the offer on the table.

What was the price if one paid to sell one's soul?

Saint steepled his fingers. His voice dropped, soft and quiet between them, captured in the space of the little booth and traveling no farther. "You think I'll give you drugs and hold your hand while you go gentle into that good night?"

"You don't look like the serial killer type. Knives and kill rooms and that sort of thing."

"Someone watches *Dexter*." Saint's smile was thin and humorless. "I'm not a serial killer. But I'm also not going to kill you. Or help you kill yourself."

"What? Then why am I here?"

"Because you want to die. I can make that happen. Indirectly, but it will happen."

Grey leaned back in his seat with a frown. "You're starting to lose me."

"Forgive me. This is the first time I've actually been honest with someone about this. I'm ... clumsy, with the truth."

"You mean before you've—"

He broke off as the barista returned. She set a fresh, steaming mug of black coffee before Saint, along with an extra sugar shaker, larger than the one on the condiment island; she fixed him with another of those looks, but he ignored her with cool, quiet dismissal, expression smoothly bland.

"Anything else I can get you gentlemen?"

"We're fine," Grey said, lips numb. "Just fine."

But she lingered. Lingered in a way that made Grey feel as if she *knew*, as if this was some kind of setup and any moment they'd be slapped in cuffs and led away. But then she shrugged and walked away again. Grey kept his eye on her until she slipped behind the counter and continued wiping it clean, while Saint blithely sipped his coffee, then set it down, picked up the sugar shaker, and dumped a steady stream of white granules into the mug.

"I know why you're looking at me that way," he said mildly. "Before you ask: no, this is not a police sting. No, I don't have a trail of medically assisted suicides in my history. However, this wouldn't be the first time someone died because of me."

Grey closed his eyes and forcibly stamped down on the rising, slow-burn heat of his sparking temper. "All right. Let's not play games. No more cryptic messages, no more dancing around the issue. Just tell me if you can help me or not."

"I'm trying, Mr. Jean-Marcelin. But it's not so simple as it seems. In order for this to happen, you must understand certain ... things."

"Such as?"

Saint abandoned the sugar shaker for a plastic stir stick, and balanced it between slim fingertips. "What if I told you I'm over two hundred years old?"

Grey sighed. "I'd remind you that you just told me you were clumsy with the truth."

"Not exactly a reason to trust me, I know." Saint twisted his lips thoughtfully. "One moment."

He set his mug and the stirrer down, then turned to rummage in the pockets of his coat. He came up with a jingling key ring, and sorted through the keys until he found a longer one with little serrated teeth. With a glance over his shoulder at the shop—the near-empty shop, no one looking in their direction—he stretched out one bare forearm against the table, then pressed the key's teeth against his skin.

Grey recoiled. "What are you—"

"Watch."

Saint raked down sharply, his tongue caught between his teeth with a hiss, a flinch tightening his shoulders. Grey reached out to stop him, heart flipping, but the key bit into Saint's arm, dug hard, scraped—and opened a jagged line of shallowly torn skin, dotted stipples of blood rising to gleam brilliant and stark against white flesh.

Grey parted his lips, started to ask *What are you doing*—but before his eyes, those paper-fine, pale tatters of skin began to melt back into place, as if rewinding the damage. The blood sank back into the skin. He stared, his tongue thick and leaden, his mouth locked in iron, as the ragged little scrape was absorbed into clean, unbroken flesh, until that slender arm was as flawless as if it had never been.

He shook his head, pushing back. His stomach jolted, shuddered. "Did—did you just—"

"Heal? Yes."

"H-how . . . ?"

"Simple." Bondye, that fucking *shrug* again. "I'm not human."

Grey just stared at him, then around the shop. A shop that didn't seem real all of a sudden, as if he'd woken up in the middle of a dream and the dream world hadn't gone away, leaving Grey the only thing *solid* in a place of imagination and twisted subconscious thoughts. He stared dully at the barista as she pulled her russet hair free from its tail, then looped it back into the tie with matter-of-fact simplicity. Mundane. Normal. As if Grey hadn't just watched Saint tear his arm open, and then heal from the wound in seconds.

Too normal.

It snapped together sharply, and he flushed hotly, mortification worming inside his chest. He'd fallen for it. Of course he'd fallen for it. He laughed bitterly, scrubbing a hand over his face.

"All right. Where are the hidden cameras?"

"No cameras. This is not a prank. Not a joke."

"What just happened, that—that isn't possible."

"I assure you, it is. And so much more." Saint wrapped his fingers around his mug and watched Grey steadily, eyes unblinking, lidded. "I am not human. Perhaps I was long ago, but not anymore. I'm over two hundred years old. I don't remember who I am, where I came from, or how I came to be this way. But if I don't take a life roughly every twenty years . . . I begin to wither and die. And the only thing I have to do to take that life is be with you."

"'Be with me,'" he repeated.

"Have a relationship with you, Mr. Jean-Marcelin." A sly smile tugged at Saint's lips. "How intimate is at your discretion."

"Oh." None of this was making sense, but as that came together, Grey's breaths sucked in roughly; that strange, cloudy feeling that had enveloped him outside the hospital came back, wrapping him in something hot and smothering that made his skin feel too warm, too tight. "*Oh.*"

"Yes," Saint mocked, curling the tip of his tongue against his plush upper lip. "'Oh.'"

"So I date you . . . and you . . . what, suck my life out just through prolonged contact?"

"That's such an inelegant way of putting it, but yes. It's not an exchange without benefits. Not only will you find the death you seek, but in your last days you'll find the inspiration I suspect you've lacked lately. Your death will come in a blaze of glory, and all will remember the work of the Grey. A much finer legacy, I think, than the one you'd intended to leave with that shotgun."

What. No. What? How— He couldn't— No. The first time he tried to speak, it didn't work. Nor the second, but finally Grey forced his tongue to move. "You're crazy."

"I'm not."

"You have to be, if you expect me to think this is real."

Saint pursed his lips. "What do you have to lose if it isn't? If I fail to drain your life, there's nothing stopping you from finding other ways."

"And if I screw it up again, I spend the rest of my life medicated in a padded cell at Memorial Health, with no memory of who I really am."

"Wouldn't that be unfortunate," Saint said flatly, then inclined his head. "I can make sure you don't fail."

"I don't believe you."

"That's your choice." Saint pushed his mug away and stood, draping his jacket over his arm. "Enjoy the rest of your evening, Mr. Jean-Marcelin. Thank you for the coffee."

He turned away. Grey stared after him, despair chewing him up inside until he felt like a ragged husk. He'd hoped for something more concrete. Something he could rely on. And maybe, yes, deep down he'd hoped for someone to hold his hand while he went gentle into that good night. To not be alone when he took his last breath.

What he'd gotten was something unreal. Something he couldn't believe.

But as Saint started to walk away, Grey felt the last of his hope slipping away with him.

He stood before he could stop himself. Before he could talk himself out of this, before he could recognize the breathless madness of it, stepping willingly off a cliff into sheer, surreal insanity because an institutional escapee had used a simple parlor trick to draw Grey into his delusional fantasy.

"Wait," he gasped, and reached for Saint's hand. Grasped his fingers, so slender and warm against his own, the skin soft and strangely smooth, fitting so *neatly* against his palm. "What if I say yes? What if I want to do it?"

Saint stopped, glancing over his shoulder. One veiled eye studied Grey.

"Before I decide," Saint said, "show me your art."

✳ 9 ✳

For some reason, he hadn't expected the pickup truck.

Saint had known dozens of artists. Some he'd loved, some he hadn't, but he'd started to define them as *types*. The Bohemian, refusing to own a car, getting around only on foot or by bike. The Modernista, trendy urbanites who had first taken hired carriages, then hired cars, then UberX cabs around brightly lit metropolises. The Folk Artist, who only drove when they borrowed their spouse's station wagon or minivan. The Urban Artist, with a slick but sensible sedan that blended neatly into any parked street. The Student Artist, getting by on pennies that were often the choice between bus fare and a ramen dinner.

He wasn't sure what type would drive a rickety, guttering, forty-year-old pickup like this, its color half blood-red rust and half flaking bits of paint that might have once been blue. Maybe Grey wasn't a type at all.

What did that make him, then, other than salvation and damnation in one?

Saint leaned against the inside door of Grey's pickup with his cheek propped against his fist, his stomach a violent nest of rattling snakes, his fingers still warm from Grey's touch. Outside the truck, the streetlights whipped past like spotlights illuminating a play set on the stage of the underworld, so thick was the late-night murk. Grey hadn't looked at him since he held the passenger-side door for him like chivalry was still a thing; he'd started the clanking engine and pulled out of the coffee shop parking lot, onto the road, with his gaze trained straight ahead and his eyes a touch glassy. The silence between them was made up half of Grey's palpable disbelief, self-doubt, mistrust.

The other half was Saint's, and he was afraid to look at it closely enough to understand it at all.

He had no idea what he was doing. What he was doing when he put on the kind of coy, enticing smiles he'd learned men liked to see; when he played the coquette, hiding safely behind the mask of someone who'd worn the mask of the seducer, the femme fatale, a thousand times before. It wasn't a game he was good at. Every other time he'd just . . . fallen, genuine and true, and fought himself over it every step of the way. He wasn't accustomed to making a performance of it. To striking a bargain.

It felt so cold. So mercenary. So careless of another life. So selfish.

And he wasn't sure he could go through with it.

Nor did he think he could stand this silence a moment longer. Was this how murderers felt before their first planned kills? Trembling and sick with it, judged by something unseen, and yet weighed down by the heavy compulsion that said he *had* to do it?

I don't want to die.

He closed his eyes, breathed in deep, then made himself look at Grey. The man stared straight ahead at the road; in the darkness, coyote yellow had deepened to a burnished, liquid shade of honey that swam with a thousand questions Saint didn't have answers to. Stark lights played in black and white planes over his gracefully sloping features and high cheekbones. His broad, angular shoulders were painfully hard, tense, deep brown skin drawn taut as a silk banner, lines of meaning written in the language of flesh.

Saint thought Grey just might be terrified.

How strange, he thought. *Someone being afraid of me, when for so long I've been afraid of myself.*

He didn't know what to say. But he had to say something, and after a moment he tried, "How is this thing even still running?"

Grey flinched. His hands squeaked on the steering wheel, then relaxed. "Luck. Hard work." He smiled faintly. "I tamper with her on weekends, or when I get blocked and need to clear my head. She's a family heirloom. My grandfather's first car, then my father's, and now mine."

"'She'?"

"People gender ships. Why can't I gender my truck?"

"Touché."

Grey glanced at him. There was a certain wildness to his eyes, that look of a man about to take a risk, take a leap, fall without knowing where the bottom was—but his voice was steady, calm, thoughtful.

"You said this is the first time you've been honest about what you are." He fixed his gaze back on the road. "But you've killed others. How?"

I wish I knew.

The pain of it was so familiar, so constant, that he almost didn't feel the fresh stab rousing the instinct to curl forward in a ball to protect himself. He forced himself to hold still, forced himself to shrug, but he couldn't stand to look at Grey anymore and instead followed the sweep of headlights over the road, picking out one yellow line after another in a ticker-tape parade.

"Just by loving them," he said. "That's all. I love them. They die."

"You're a black widow."

He closed his eyes. "Something like that."

Grey remained silent, the only sound his shaky, uncertain breath, and then, "I'm sorry."

Such simple words. And yet Saint could almost believe Grey meant them, from the soft, hesitant emotion in his voice, the heaviness in the air between him.

What kind of man could feel pity for the man who would be his killer?

"Don't," he said. "Don't feel sorry for me. I don't deserve it."

"Why not?"

"I kill everyone I'm stupid enough to care for."

"That," Grey said, "is exactly why you deserve it."

Saint wrapped his arms around himself. When he landed on this crazy idea, he hadn't wanted . . . *this.* Hadn't wanted to look at Grey and see someone who made him think maybe, just maybe, he might need those strong, dark arms wrapped around him and easing the pain he'd kept a secret inside himself for centuries. Not even with the others had he been able to take comfort. Not when everything that was happening to them was his fault, and he couldn't tell them. Not if he wanted to survive.

And he couldn't take comfort in Grey. He couldn't think Grey would offer, based on a few kind words spoken while the man was probably still in shock. And even if he did . . .

Saint had to keep this strictly business. It was just a transaction. Nothing else.

"It's not your burden," he said, forcing his voice to remain steady, trying to feel cold inside so that Grey would see cold outside. "It's only your choice if you want to take on that role."

"'Come into my parlor,' said the spider to the fly."

"Don't be clever."

"My apologies." The shivering rumble of the engine quieted. "We're here."

Grey eased the pickup truck into a curbside parking spot amid the urban kitsch of the Savannah City Market, trendy retro-modern bars bumping up against historic buildings draped in street art that shone misty in the understated streetlamps. If Saint remembered correctly, the tall, white-fronted building across the square housed multiple art galleries; he hadn't been here in ages, preferring to avoid the Market scene. There were too many lovely, passionate young talents who clustered here, and the last thing he wanted was to feel that *pull* again, the fire of their creation waiting to be bled from them and absorbed into himself. Sometimes he wondered if it wasn't the men he fell in love with but the addictive allure of that *glow* inside them, the mystery of how they took the human soul and gave it life as something tangible that others could consume.

Before Saint could even unbuckle his seat belt, Grey had slipped out of the driver's seat and circled the truck to open the passenger-side door for him. Saint eyed him dryly, then sighed and climbed out of the truck. Grey tossed his head and turned to lead him across the square; Saint slipped his hands into his pockets and trailed after.

"It's after four in the morning. Are we even allowed to be here?"

"Most of the long-term artists have keys. We come in to do setup work before the galleries open to the public, or to help out with upkeep."

The scent of magnolias sweltered on the air, heavy, crushing down on him as he followed Grey in silence. He would always remember this night by the scent of magnolias, he thought, and wondered if every summer when they bloomed he would think of the night he'd finally broken and become some kind of monster.

Grey let them into the darkened building, slipping the chain padlock with a key, then led him up an exposed spiral staircase and walkway looking out over open suites of clustered galleries, shops, and display rooms. Their steps echoed on the white tile, the only sounds save the distant hush of the central air; their reflections swam dimly beneath them, mirrored in the floors like ghosts haunting the eerily quiet, empty building. There was something deeply personal about being here right now: just the two of them, drifting through this place like echoes that would vanish with the coming of the day and the waking world.

Grey hesitated in front of a pair of sliding glass doors. Saint stopped a few feet behind him, studying the stiff line of his spine.

"Something wrong?"

"No." Grey shook his head. "Nothing."

Liar, Saint thought, but kept his mouth shut.

Grey unlocked the glass doors and pushed them aside, then stepped in. The lights came up in dim spots, positioned to highlight various art installations scattered about a large, spare room with tasteful minimalism: white pedestals supporting translucent glass sculptures, hanging installations in pure, shimmering motes of LED light making illusory shapes of dragonflies and cicadas and scarabs.

Saint lingered before a painting of a city of twisted, dark warrens in lurid neon colors against black, littered with Chinese characters. The plaque below read, *The Walled City – Marci Lebreaux*, and sparked a memory of a time long ago: the smell of opium and the shadows of close, lightless warrens. He traced his fingers lightly over the engraved brushed steel, then followed Grey into a dim-lit back room lined wall-to-wall with figures dripping with paint and seeming to scoff at the idea that they were only *art*.

The first impression Saint had was of being embraced by shadows, as if Grey had tapped into some vein of the night's black blood, and used it to paint the massive floor-to-ceiling canvases. Grey's hot amber eyes looked out from each one: intense, deep-sunk, set in the shadows of a face painted in sharp, geometric slashes of black and gray and blue, touched with highlights of blood red and twilight violet that shivered with the violent, latent energy of something dark; something that tried to reach off the canvas and touch him with the intimacy of all the secret, terrible thoughts people never shared with anyone else. There was something almost brutal to the brushstrokes, Saint thought. As if Grey was punishing the version of himself that lived on the canvas, captured in a half-dozen angles that highlighted the starkness of his features, the extremes of an elegant, almost regal profile, the fullness of his lips sealed tight as if holding a scream inside.

Saint drifted closer to a piece that took up an entire wall, a profile of Grey looking up at something off-canvas, his expression somewhere between supplication, despair, and hatred. Saint reached out to delicately touch the painting, feeling the faint, subtle ridges of the brushstrokes through the dried oil paints, the texture of the canvas, as he traced the low slope of his nose, down to the pronounced dip beneath, over the shapes of his lips.

What did Grey hate so much? What was he looking at, in this painting?

"These aren't real," Grey said at his side, startling his heart into a racing little fillip. He glanced over at Grey, who stood with his hands in his pockets, looking up at the portrait with that same lost, searching sense of loathing, poorly hidden by the lightness of his tone. "Not really. I didn't feel anything when I painted them. But I had a deadline, a showing, my agent waiting. Sometimes bills trump artistic inspiration."

"You don't like painting yourself."

"I don't like seeing myself." Grey reached out to flick his painted doppelgänger's forehead; his fingernail made a soft *thock* against the canvas. "Or maybe I just don't like seeing my demons on display for everyone to see. Maybe I just say it's not real because I don't like what's looking back at me."

"When was the last time you felt inspired, Mr. Jean-Marcelin?"

Grey glanced down. When their eyes met, Saint almost recoiled; he didn't understand why Grey was watching him that way, as if his face were as much a portrait as these paintings, baring everything inside him for Grey to consume in all its hues.

"Grey," his dark, soft lips said. "Please call me Grey."

Saint licked his lips. He suddenly felt the cold of the air conditioning too much, his skin too hot against it. "Grey, then."

That full mouth twitched into an imitation of a smile; then Grey turned away. "The last time . . ." He sighed. "I don't know. The market series, I think."

"Show me those."

"They're not here. They're at my place." He toyed with one of the belt loops of his jeans. "I . . . I took them out of the galleries. I didn't want anyone to see them."

"Why not?"

"I'm not really sure." Grey canted a glance toward him. "Why do you want to see them? What are you hoping to find?"

"I can't explain. I'll know it when I see it." Saint turned away—from the haunting gaze on the canvas, from the haunted gaze that questioned him. "Just . . . show me."

✳⋲ 10 ⋺✳

Show me, Saint said, and Grey lingered on the supple line of his back, on the way his hair feathered and licked at the nape of his neck, the slope of his throat fascinating.

What do you want from me, Saint?

Why do you need to see me naked this way, if only to see that mine is a life worth ending?

The slender, lovely man was already walking away. Grey almost didn't follow. Almost ended this right here. Saint was playing some kind of game with him, one that would leave him unsatisfied and still lost, trying to find his way into the dark. The idea of baring his inner self to this man only to be left by the wayside was repellent.

And yet the way Saint had touched the canvas, the way he'd said Grey's name . . .

Some part of him wanted Saint to see. Wanted to be *known* that way by this fey, strange man.

How would it feel, then, when Saint brushed his fingertips over canvas that might as well be Grey's living flesh?

He shuddered and stepped away from the gallery, from the towering, judgmental faces of his mirror selves, waiting to cast him into the afterlife—where he would spend his year and a day trapped, before Bawon Samedi would let him free on the wind. His own gaze followed him, spearing into him, asking him what he was doing as he caught up with Saint, brushed his arm, stepped ahead.

"Come on," he said, and flicked his fingers. "I'll take you there."

✳⟞ 11 ⟝✳

This time, Saint didn't bother breaking the silence in the truck. Not when he knew with a sick certainty that whatever it was that called out to him . . . it was in Grey. He'd felt it on his skin in a shivering spark when he touched those painted lips, and wondered in that low, quiet part of himself how those lips would taste, how they would feel yielding and soft against his own.

It wasn't just about base attraction. No doubt Grey was beautiful: ebonwood and silver and gold, agile grace paired with a delicate blend of power and elegance that made him more striking in motion than any painting of him could ever be.

But Saint needed more than the physical. One-night stands, purely sexual relationships, had never done anything for him. Never given him what he needed, never left his lover wilting like a morning glory under the noonday sun. He didn't know if this intuitive sense was some instinct belonging to whatever kind of *thing* he was, singling out his prey . . . or just the simplicity of a real human connection, perverted by his terrible needs.

He only knew it was there when he looked at Grey, and felt his palms burn with the want to reach out and take his hand.

Grey drove them to an industrial block overlooking the Savannah River, warehouses and factories interspersed neatly with former cousins now converted to apartments. They parked outside the long, tall block of a rehabbed factory building that still had the old pipe smokestack on the roof, stark contrast to the trendy little wrought-iron balconies that had likely been tacked on in the last decade or two. Inside, a wide, rattling cage of a freight elevator gave room for them to stand at opposite ends, staring at the walls, the numbers, anything but each other.

On the top floor, the mesh-grating door lifted and let them out into a massive single-room apartment space: two terraced levels a couple of feet apart in height and joined by short steps, floors paneled in gleaming cherrywood, walls of old brick mixed with new, deliberately tarnished to make it look aged. The far wall was nothing but a bank of floor-to-ceiling windows, looking out over the night-dark gleam of the river and, on the far side, the line of shimmering city lights that marked the river's bank.

The furnishings were quiet, minimalist, lit by subtly spaced, deep amber lamps; the exposed-beam ceilings arched so high that Saint's steps echoed faintly as he slipped inside, turning, taking it all in. He hadn't had time before, in the minute it had taken to check Grey's vitals, get him on a stretcher, and wheel him into the back of an ambulance. Now, in the quiet of the night, without red and blue flashing lights and the scream of sirens, he felt like an intruder in Grey's space, demanding to be brought into the privacy of his home.

He stopped, though, as his gaze landed on a dark stain on the floor. Right in the middle, as if the blood had been pooling there for so long that not even the lacquered finish could stop it from soaking into the wood.

He cleared his throat and looked away. "Must every artist in the world have a tastefully decorated industrial loft?"

That coaxed a smile from Grey's lips. "I do have an image to uphold."

At the far end of the room, on the upper terrace where a wide platform bed had been tucked against the brick, Saint caught sight of a tapestry hanging low on the wall: small, no larger than a handkerchief, in a pale, reddish violet embroidered with black stitches, forming a stylized heart cut through with swooping, curling lines, crosses, and stars. Below it, set atop a carved wooden box lacquered black and engraved with the same design, were several candles in glass jars painted with the heart pattern, scattered among incense holders empty of everything but soft gray piles of ash. He frowned, trying to place where he'd seen something like that before.

"Voodoo?" he asked, turning back to Grey.

"Catholic vodou." The man shrugged almost sheepishly and climbed the steps, drifting toward the little altar. "I'm no houngan. Barely vodouisant. Just the third-generation son of an immigrant family from Port-au-Prince. I can barely speak Kreyole, and my accent is terrible."

As they drew closer, Saint caught a subtle difference in the floor just in front of the altar: faint twin depressions of darker wood, the polish worn off. Grey had knelt here many times before. "But you honor the old ways."

"My granmé's ways." A compelling, sweet warmth softened Grey's voice. "You know vodou?"

"No. But when you've been alive as long as I have, you pick up interesting little details here and there. I didn't know practitioners of the faith kept shrines in their homes."

Grey sank to one knee before the altar and reached out to trace the pattern on the tapestry. "This is a veve. Like a shrine, but . . . it is more an open door, a place for the loa to make your home their home, to tell them where to find you. This one is to Erzulie. Erzulie Freda, in her rada aspect."

He followed the shapes of the design with a familiarity that bordered on ritual, the brush of his fingers as slow and sensuous as a touch to a lover's skin. Saint caught himself watching, and looked away with a sharp rush of heat burning the tips of his ears.

"She is a decadent creature, deeply sexual," Grey continued, the rumble of his voice husky. "The lady of the moon. She loves beauty in all things, and so she gives those who love her the ability to create beauty for her. I give her my love and open my home to her; I put my gifts to her inside this box. In return, she gives me the gift of my talent."

The familiarity of it struck hard, struck deep, enough to chase that flush away and leave Saint cold. "By that logic . . . does that make me a loa?"

"If you are truly not human . . ." Grey lifted his gaze to him, those golden eyes stark, almost hunting him. "Perhaps a loa is acting through you."

Saint took a few steps back and nearly tripped over the steps, his heel tottering. With a soft sound and a jolt of his stomach, he caught himself—then turned away quickly, even if he felt far too vulnerable giving his back to Grey.

"Show me the paintings," he said thickly.

The faint scuff of Grey's footsteps drew closer. His body heat prickled at Saint's back.

"Come," Grey murmured, the rolling depths of his voice shivering into Saint's ear, and he sucked in a sharp breath.

Then Grey brushed past him, arm trailing along his, and he was gone, walking away and leaving Saint trembling, petrified, and wondering why he could still feel the curl of Grey's breaths wisping his hair from the nape of his neck.

The far side of the apartment had been walled off by a heavy black curtain. Grey threw it aside on a scene of chaos. Half-finished canvases propped everywhere; empty paint-smeared cans held brushes of every shape and size, stacked on windowsills and carts and tables and on the floor, pinning down drop cloths stained in every color under the rainbow. Crumpled tubes of paint lay about as if they'd exploded from a piñata. Saint arched a brow, crossing carefully into a chaos that was as different from the apartment's peace as night and day, all the lived-in turmoil that was absent from the rest of the space absolutely evident here.

Grey dragged away the protective cloth covering a series of canvases leaning against the windows: long, low, painted so that they fitted end-to-end to create one continuous scene, and Saint was once again struck by that sensation of being embraced by shadows.

No, of being *submerged* in shadow, as if each canvas were not a flat picture but a window reaching into a three-dimensional world of night captured within the bubble of the painting. Grey had chosen to paint in paler shades on black canvas—the suggestion of light glinting off a curving shoulder or shining from red-painted lips, offering the fluidity of black bodies moving with such grace against an endless night. They crowded among market stalls decked out in bone and feathers and beads; strings of organs dangled from the canopies of ultraviolet umbrellas, pulsing hearts casting red light like lanterns, lungs breathing on their cords. People traded with shopkeepers who were never quite human—always some small thing giving them away beyond the unearthly beauty of full lips and flat noses and angled eyes and sculpted cheekbones, strong shoulders and curving hips and swaying breasts. Glowing cat's eyes. Foreheads sprouting delicate horns. Fingers replaced by the long, curling legs of a spider, and braids a crown of tiny, twined serpents. They took jewelry and ears of corn and rabbits and human fingers and eyes, and traded back little tied-up pouches that burned from inside with the colors of a million emotions.

And there *was* emotion here—so much more than the self-loathing and despair that Saint had seen in those gallery paintings. The richness of a complex and tumultuous heart that changed with every shift in the winds, with every which way life pushed it, as if captured on these canvases was everything a man might feel in his life, from birth through to a sharp and sudden death. And for just a moment, as Saint took in the delicate brushstrokes alternating with such harsh, powerful lines, he felt something deeper than skin. Something familiar, a deep and ancient memory that resonated with knowledge he'd once known and long forgotten. As if he was connected to the source of an alien life force, stirring and rich and terrifying, a vast thing where all he'd ever known first originated, peering out from its secret shadows.

"This is where your heart is," he breathed.

"Mm," Grey agreed, and moved to stand at his side, their arms brushing. "I meant it to be Haiti. The Haiti in my heart. I've never been. But I know it like I know the loa. Like I know home."

"Would you like to go, someday?"

Grey turned his head, looking down at him, studying him intently. "I'm not really thinking in terms of 'someday.'"

Saint trembled and pulled away. He couldn't do this if Grey said things like that, if he reminded him with every moment just what this meant. He tore his gaze away from those questioning eyes and focused on the painting, on the detail of a voluptuous woman with a close-cropped cap of hair and goat's hooves for feet parting the folds of her pregnant belly as if opening a pomegranate, to let a weeping woman reach inside to extract the shining jewel of the fat, smiling baby within.

"What does it all mean?"

"In Port-au-Prince, where my granmé was from, there are these markets. She would tell me about them: crowds and noise, and scents of dust and green things freshly picked. Bushels and bales and buckets lining the streets under colorful umbrellas, the kamlo all shouting, 'Look at me, look at me, buy my wares, feed my family.'" He let go of the pitched accent and chuckled, curling his hand against the top of one canvas. "You trade. You trade money, or goods, or services. Always trade. Always haggle. Like the vodouisant with the loa."

"What are the loa, really?"

"The spirits of vodou. The rada. The petro. The ghede lwa, the envoi mort." His voice rolled over the names with a quiet worship, caressing them with his soft, curving lips. "The gods of vodou, they are mercenary ones. Practical. But not evil, as America's movies like to paint them; they are forces of nature, not to be judged by human ideas of good and evil. They are the gods of a people who trade not in dreams and grand designs, but in day-to-day survival. But they are not gods without hearts. They enjoy your faith, your worship, but they like your gifts more. In exchange, they trade in what you wish. What you desire. Even if it may not always come to you as you please."

Grey's voice captured him, held him, until its low, hypnotic cadence became a part of the paintings, leading Saint through the rows of market stalls, discovering new details every time he looked. So caught was he in its richness, its fullness, that he didn't realize how close Grey was until he lifted his head—and stilled as he found the man looking down at him, Grey's chest a hair's breadth from brushing his shoulder. His stomach quaked. He bit his lip, looking up into those angled, expressive eyes that were telling him something he didn't understand.

"So this is the dark market of the loa," he whispered. "Trading in human desire."

Grey's low sound of assent was lost in the thundering of Saint's heart as the man leaned closer. Body to body, warmth to warmth, his lips and breath stirring Saint's hair with every hushed word.

"Are you human enough to know desire?"

"Yes. I know." Saint's voice nearly broke. He didn't know what this shivering moment was, how it had fallen upon them like a cloak to enshroud them in a shared secret and draw him closer. Closer to the magnetic pulse of Grey's body. Closer to the inviting curves of his lips. Closer to the very human pulse of *desire*, and if he dared, if he closed that last distance . . . "I know it far too well, Grey Jean-Marcelin."

✳⛫ 12 ⛫✳

Grey looked down into dusk-shadowed eyes framed by lush, trembling lashes. Eyes that looked up at him with something raw and unguarded inside, something that belonged to the real man who called himself Saint instead of the enticing, mocking act he'd strung Grey along with. Something that ignited a *need* inside him, pulling him with a dark and drugged fire, until he couldn't put together a single thought except the desire to taste the pink bow of pale lips. He felt fever-sick with it, too hot inside, fire rising up to cloud his brain and take control of his limbs.

He lifted his hands, reached for Saint, aching to enclose narrow hips in the grip of his fingers—but Saint flinched back, stumbling, breaking the fragile thread stretching between them. The air rushed back into Grey's lungs, and he backed away, taking several slow, calming breaths.

"Sorry," he ground out. "Sorry."

Saint stared at him, almost accusatory—before his face shuttered over as if he'd painted on his mocking little smile with a practiced hand, *that fucking shrug* lifting his shoulders. "I told you."

"Are . . . are you doing this to me?"

"I don't know. Am I?"

Grey shook his head. His fingers shook. "Don't. Don't . . . *do* things to me."

"I'm not doing anything at all." Saint turned away with one last taunting glance over his shoulder. "Because you don't think this is real."

Grey set his jaw, a glare pinching around his eyes, but Saint ignored him and sank to a crouch in front of the paintings, studying them with a quietly absorbed intensity. Grey almost wanted to cover them again, pull Saint away from them, refuse to let him look. His soul was in these paintings more than any self-portraits depicting clichéd expressions of anguish. These images were his roots, the clay and blood that shaped him into a man, the elements that crafted his chemical composition. He'd put everything into the smallest detail, hiding his secrets in the ringlet of hair waxed to a smooth black cheek and the veve symbol worked into the seal on a golden signet ring.

And when Saint stroked his fingertips over the painted lines, moving as if he was letting the faint raised lines of the oils lead him over the slope of Maman Brigitte's shoulder, it felt to Grey as if he'd stroked low down in Grey's belly, touching somewhere below his heart and where the most primal parts of him lived.

Was it real? How else could he explain this visceral reaction to Saint? He didn't even *know* the man, yet every minute he spent in his company gutted him and threatened to cut through the dulling filter he'd lived with for so long, to burn him with the harshness of a light he couldn't stand. If he was really some kind of . . . psychic vampire or whatever, maybe he gave off an aura that ensnared his targets. Swayed their perceptions, lowered their resistance, forced an unnatural reaction.

Is this unnatural, this attraction?

And are you really starting to buy into this?

Saint's hand fell from the canvas, and he stood. "You're quite talented. These are beautiful. Painted in heart's blood," he said softly, then cast Grey a veiled sidelong glance. "Yes. I think this can work."

"Just like that?" He avoided meeting Saint's eyes directly. As if that could protect him, somehow, from the alluring effect. "So what? Am I supposed to paint you now?"

Saint scoffed under his breath. "Don't bore me. I'm not that kind of muse."

"Then how does it work?"

"We just . . . have to be close. Date like anyone else would. Being around me will act as . . ." A soft, sultry laugh, far too practiced. "As ridiculous as it sounds, I'm like jumper cables for your creativity. I shock it into overdrive, but once you turn up the dials, you can't turn them back down. It will burn you out. Consume you with a wasting sickness. You die. I live."

Grey suddenly remembered where he'd heard something similar before. "Like a leanan sidhe."

Saint's stillness was so sudden and absolute, it was as if some great hand had grasped him and crushed him to the spot. His head snapped up, and he stared at Grey. "You know that story?"

"Read it in a book of fairy tales somewhere. Makes sense, really."

Saint's brow furrowed. He shook his head. "But . . . the leanan sidhe is a woman."

"Says who? Stories told by men who think only women have deep responses to emotional trauma?" He snorted. "It's the twenty-first century. Girls can be astronauts. Boys can be jilted fairy vampires."

But Saint just . . . *looked* at him. Like he'd cut open some raw wound and stuck his fingers deep inside, raking hard into the vulnerable flesh of him to leave him bleeding. Fuck. Fuck, he hadn't even thought— Sometimes it was too easy to take that flippancy for truth, when probably— *Fuck*.

How much did it have to hurt to not know who or what you were, and the only guess you had was spelled out in a two-hundred-year trail of bodies?

"I'm sorry." He stepped closer, started to reach for him again, stopped. "I don't mean to make light. Sometimes the gallows humor goes a little too far."

"It's not that, I just . . ."

"Just what?"

Saint shivered, and wrapped his arms around himself as if to ward against a chill. "I'm wondering if I was once human, or if I never was at all."

"That's not what I'd wonder."

"What would you wonder, then?"

This time, when the urge came to reach out, Grey didn't stop himself. He caught a lock of soft black hair, its cool texture pouring between his fingers like water, and curled it against Saint's cheek.

"I," he murmured, "would wonder who hurt you enough to make you this way."

✳ 13 ✳

This wasn't how it was supposed to work.

Saint wasn't supposed to break like this. Wasn't supposed to crack open so much that Grey, a stranger, his *victim*, could read him so easily. This was the danger of telling the truth to someone else, when he'd spent so many years avoiding even acknowledging the truth *himself*. So many years in denial—denial that had killed so many men, that had told him he wasn't a murderer as long as he didn't do it on purpose, as long as he was just trying to ease his selfish loneliness.

And now here Grey was, looking at him, *seeing* him, and calling him leanan sidhe. He couldn't be. He didn't *want* to be, when it meant he was . . . was . . .

Cursed.

If the books had been right, when he'd first looked all those years ago, searching for his answers . . . either a mortal or a sidhe woman, brokenhearted and betrayed by a lover, could gain enough power to become a vengeful fae spirit. Only the circumstances had to be very specific: the lover had to abandon them not just for another woman, but for his passion, scorning his love for his work. And so the leanan sidhe preyed on artists, on creative energy, feeding them exactly what they prized so deeply, but at a price. Punishing them for their passion, yet making it burn brighter than it ever could on its own.

But if that was what he was . . .

How?

Why didn't he *remember*?

And who had done this to him, cursing him to this life as if *he* somehow deserved to be punished?

I didn't do anything wrong!

It came from somewhere deep and awful inside him, a cry of certainty without the memories to back it up. As quickly as it rose inside him, he pushed it away; just because Grey suggested it, didn't make it *true*. Just because Grey offered a different perspective to something Saint had outright rejected, didn't make it *right*.

He pulled fiercely away from the other man, breathing hard, staring into those soft golden eyes that seemed to offer compassion, understanding—when Grey knew enough about him to hate him more than any of the pretty men he'd lied to so he could love them for just a little while longer.

He buried his fingers in his hair, then turned away quickly, staring toward the window. "I . . . I think I need a drink."

Grey made a low sound, then fell silent for a few heavy beats before asking, "Alcoholic, or non?"

"Non. Please." He choked on a laugh. "You don't want me drunk right now."

He stared fixedly out the window, listening while Grey's footsteps moved away, followed by the sounds of the refrigerator door opening, ice tinkling in glasses, liquid pouring, the refrigerator door closing again. Then those steps returned—too soon, not nearly enough time for Saint to compose himself and ease the painful knot in his chest.

Grey drifted into his peripheral vision and offered a tall glass of something translucent and golden. "Iced green tea."

"Thank you."

He took the glass, careful not to brush Grey's fingers, and cupped it in both hands to let the cool, slick condensation chill his palms. When he took a sip it was faintly bitter, faintly sweet, a touch of tartness, the flavors delicate. He focused on that rather than the man at his side, watching him with a sense of quiet expectation. Saint swallowed and dared a glance at Grey.

"You're starting to believe me, aren't you?"

"Maybe. I'm not sure."

"What made you stop thinking this was a prank?"

"Other than not being able to figure out how you'd fake healing a wound?"

"Fake the wound itself. Corn-syrup blood and a thin layer of synthetic skin."

Grey arched a brow. "I thought you *wanted* me to believe you."

"I want you to work through the rational possibilities and see the flaws in them. For instance . . . if I cut false skin and fake blood, where did the synthetic skin go when you were watching me the entire time and I never peeled it away? Why weren't there any bloodstains left behind?"

"All right. That's one option out the window." Gray sighed and sipped his own tea, looking out over the view. "What about pheromone cologne?"

"What?"

"I mean . . . that . . . the thing you do."

He blinked. "I don't know what you're talking about."

"Don't you— Never mind." A stain of red flushed Grey's dark skin even darker. He cleared his throat. "Aren't you afraid?"

"Of what?"

"Being discovered."

He smiled bitterly. "I have more years of experience keeping my secrets than you have minutes of knowing them, Grey."

"But I could expose you."

"And who would believe you?"

"That's cold, Saint." Grey's brows lowered thunderously; he flung Saint a recriminating look. "Is that why you picked me? Is that what you think of me? So crazy and unbalanced that no one would ever believe me?"

Oh. Oh, *shit*, he was so stupid. He shook his head quickly. "No. No, I didn't mean it that way, I—"

"Still felt that way." Grey pressed his lips together so hard Saint could see the imprints of his teeth pushing on them from the inside. "That's what everyone thinks. That's how the nurses looked at me. That's why I was afraid to survive. Because suddenly everything you do, feel, think, say, *believe* becomes suspect, just because no one understands why you'd want to die. So you just . . . must not be rational. You can't be trusted to know your own mind."

"I . . . I'm sorry."

God, he was fucking this all up. They hadn't even managed to settle on this, and already they were stabbing at each other's hurts and peeling open their most painful parts. Had he really thought he was going to be some kind of angel of mercy for a man who wanted to die? All he was turning out to be was an angel of misery, and for his arrogance, he was screwing things up for both of them.

He drifted tentatively closer and, before he could talk himself out of it, curled his hand against Grey's arm. The hard bunch of muscle pushed against his palm, warm through the thin fabric of Grey's shirt, unyielding in its tension.

"Grey." He squeezed gently, as if he could coax that stiffness to relax. "I really am sorry. I didn't mean to treat you as if you were somehow *less*."

Grey remained silent for far too long, his fierce, angry gaze staring blankly straight ahead, when Saint wished for just a moment the man would look at *him*.

But when he finally did, Saint almost couldn't stand the stark hurt chiseled across his face in dark, unforgiving lines.

"Just don't do it again," Grey growled, and pulled away.

14

Grey dumped his tea out in the sink. He didn't want it anymore, not when his stomach was a churn of feelings he couldn't quite untangle. Why did it matter if this . . . this pale, drifting ghost of a man with his crazy stories thought he was just as weak and pathetic as everyone at that hospital? Everyone who'd looked at him with pity. With *recrimination*. As if he'd offended them personally, and disgusted them in the process. Fuck, his agent hadn't even called after he was released from the hospital. Just a terse email to let him know she'd made sure the story, when it leaked to the news, was buried in a back-page side column with a brief, uninformative headline. Her terseness had said everything:

What the hell is wrong with you, Grey? What kind of worthless, spineless loser are you?

He closed his eyes, gripping the edge of the sink. Maybe that wasn't what she was thinking, but it was what the voice inside his head told him. Maybe he should just . . . check himself into Memorial. Voluntary commitment. Maybe the screws were so loose in his head he really couldn't be trusted with simple decisions—let alone the massive decision to Kevorkian himself while Saint showed him the way down into the dark.

In exchange, they trade in what you wish. What you desire. Even if it may not always come to you as you please.

Was this the lady Erzulie's answer to his prayers, then? Had she sent the hand of Bawon Samedi to his door, acting through Saint's soft, warm touch?

Whatever he expected, it hadn't been to feel that touch a moment later: slim hands against his back, snaring in his shirt, Saint's body pressing against him with a sweet, yielding heat, Saint's cheek resting between his shoulder blades. He sucked in a breath, his entire body tightening with a whip's lash of sparking, heightened awareness, until he could feel Saint's heartbeat pulsing through the contact and into his flesh.

"This is your decision," Saint whispered. Every movement of Saint's lips teased the cotton of Grey's shirt against his spine, and his shaking fingers clutched harder against the edge of the sink. "I'm not trying to manipulate you. Not trying to deceive you. Not trying to take advantage of you. You have a need. So do I. I'm trusting you to know what you want before I give it to you."

Grey closed his eyes, his head bowing. "You don't know me. Why are you offering this to me?"

"Because I want to." Saint's cheek rubbed against his back, and Grey shivered. "Because I don't think anyone else can."

He turned, gently dislodging Saint's grip and twisting to face him. Some deep part of him hoped those white doves of hands would find a new home fluttering to perch against his chest, resting graceful and pretty with their twisting black designs licking toward his fingers . . . but they only fell to Saint's side. Yet even without those hands pressed close, Saint's body layered against him with a delicate touch, barely the slightest pressure of his weight and yet enough to leave Grey warm, aching. He searched that elfin face, searching for any hint of dishonesty, of artifice, but he saw only shadowed eyes and trembling lashes and parted lips, and a silence he didn't know how to fill.

He looked away, dragging in a deep breath, forcing a smile. "This still sounds like a really creative strategy to get laid."

"Trust me," Saint said, "you aren't that hot."

He laughed—a quick, sharp bark, but it eased the tension between them and unraveled the knot that had tightened in his chest. Saint leaned back, running his fingers through his hair, leaving Grey missing his warmth.

"Thanks for the ego check," he muttered dryly. "It just seems so weird. To start a relationship like a contract."

"If it's easier for you to think of it as a contract, you can." Saint folded his arms over his chest, hunching into his shoulders. "Which I suppose makes me yours, bought and paid for."

"Don't. Don't say it that way."

"What way?"

"Like you've been bought with no choice in the matter. Like you're selling your love for nothing."

Saint peeked up at him through his lashes. "Is your life such a cheap price to pay?"

"It . . . feels that way to me."

Grey risked touching him, brushing his fingers through that dark hair, and was rewarded by a soft cheek pressing to the underside of his wrist and rubbing like an affection-starved cat, Saint's eyes lidding in a way that made his heart skip hot and hard—something he'd always wanted to feel, but had barely touched at one remove. This . . . this was attraction, then.

And he was well and truly ensnared.

"My life to save yours," he murmured, and felt a sense of acceptance settle over him. Peace. "That's a better reason to die, I think."

"You still won't tell me why you did it, will you?"

"I'm still not sure you're not more certifiable than I am."

"If it doesn't work, you can kick my bloody ass." Saint's lips twitched.

"And if it does . . . I won't be here to."

Saint stiffened, pulled away. ". . . Yeah."

Don't. Don't do it. But Grey caught himself reaching for him as if he could somehow comfort him, ease that pensive, cynical mask of forced diffidence away. He wanted the reality back, he realized. The vulnerable, broken reality that Saint only let him glimpse for short seconds before walling it off again. If he was going to be bound into this, he didn't want his last days to be tied to a painted-on smile and a dismissive shrug.

But Saint stepped out of his reach, drawing in on himself protectively, watching him with a careful wariness. Grey sighed, slumping against the edge of the sink and letting his arms drop.

"Doing this bothers you, doesn't it?"

"I'm a parasite," Saint bit off.

"Everyone has to live. People have to eat. You just happen to eat other people."

Saint sniffed, staring off to one side. "How macabre."

"I deal in the macabre, Saint. You've seen my art." *You've seen me on the floor, blood pooling everywhere, the shotgun slipping from my limp, nerveless fingers.* "How long does it take?"

"Two months. Perhaps three." Saint hesitated, then asked, "Can you stand to wait that long?"

"Three months is nothing after thirty-seven years. Or two hundred." He fidgeted, drumming his fingers against his thigh. "Is there . . . some kind of ritual to seal this, or something?"

"I don't *know*," Saint hissed. "I . . . It just happens. It was just something I fell into before. No rituals. Just . . ."

"Falling in love," Grey finished softly.

Saint closed his eyes. "Yeah. Something like that."

"Do you think you could love me?"

"I don't even *know* you."

"That is a problem."

"So we're at an impasse." Saint squared his shoulders, lifted his chin, and looked Grey dead in the eye. "Fine, then. Kiss me."

His eyes widened. His heart stopped. And for just an instant he could feel it: the shape of Saint's lips pressed to his own, the warm, wet tip of his tongue, a taste that might be crisp green apples or might be burned caramel or might be both. The weight of how much he wanted that taste to become real rocked him, hard and rough and trembling through him with desire.

And that was exactly the reason he couldn't do it.

"No," he said.

Saint blinked, then scowled. "It won't work without some kind of intimacy, Grey."

"I can handle intimacy." It was his turn to shrug. "But I don't like lies. I don't like feeling like I'm forcing you into contact, either. If I'm going to kiss you, I want to kiss *you*. Willingly. Not a martyr who's enduring my touch. And not that . . . coquettish little face you like to put on."

Sunset eyes narrowed. "How do you know that 'coquettish little face,' as you call it, isn't the real me?"

"Because you slip. Maybe you've been wearing this mask a long time. Maybe it's just a part of this merry game you're leading me on, for whatever amusement you get out of making me believe this." He cupped Saint's cheeks in his palms, catching him like catching a dragonfly before it could flutter away, gently tipping his face up. "But either way . . . it's cracking."

Saint's lips trembled. "H-how . . . how can you tell?"

"That's what I do. I see the heart of things that isn't on the surface, and paint it." He traced his thumb against the dip of smooth, warm skin pinning the corner of Saint's mouth, and savored the man's soft intake of breath. "If I'm going to kiss you, I want to see the heart of you."

"No—no, you don't—"

"I do."

A quiet sound, almost a whimper, escaped Saint's lips. "Don't fall in love with me, Grey."

"Isn't that what the leanan sidhe does? Makes his victim love him?"

"*I'm not a leanan sidhe!*" Saint snarled, tearing back from his grip, putting a distance between them that Grey couldn't stand. He looked so small, so fragile, standing there with his hands curled into trembling fists and his pretty face screwed up into what tried to be a glare and instead seemed more like the fight to repress tears. "You don't have to love me. You shouldn't love me. I'm a terrible person to love."

"You're pretending to be proud of that. You're not."

"What?"

Grey sighed, frustration a hard knot in the pit of his stomach. "I told you. I don't like lies. You come to me playing the seductive little wastrel, all knowing eyes and cool smiles, but that's not who you are."

"I don't *know* who I am. Maybe that's the truth of me."

"Then it doesn't hurt, killing people this way?"

Saint lifted his chin, a proud, stubborn tilt. "Maybe it won't this time."

"Maybe," Grey said. "Maybe you're my angel of mercy."

"I don't know what I am." Saint's mouth folded into a bitter downward turn, and he turned away. "But I know I'm nobody's angel."

He swept toward the freight elevator. That was it, then. He was leaving. Grey wondered if his chance was leaving with him, or if this was just the two of them going to their corners while they figured out how to make this work together. A small, quiet voice inside him was starting to panic at the idea of never seeing Saint again—but the numbness was descending once more, the numbness and the exhaustion, until he barely had the energy to make himself speak.

"Tell me something, Saint."

Saint stopped, his hand resting against the wall over the elevator button. "What?" he asked, the single word cold, acidic.

"If the others didn't know . . . why did you tell me?"

"Because I don't want this to be about love anymore." Saint flung a look over his shoulder, sharp as knives, yet his eyes glistened, wet and sheened. "It's just about staying alive."

Grey didn't know what to say to that. Not when he was the last person who could possibly understand a compulsion to live. But then it didn't matter, when the elevator door lifted and Saint stepped inside. The last Grey saw of him was the cage door closing, and one more flashing look before it disappeared down, down, ever down, as if sinking its way into hell. Saint was gone.

And Grey didn't know if he wanted him to come back.

✳ 15 ✳

Saint barely made it home—stumbling in the predawn dark, walking stubbornly by the side of the road instead of calling a cab or finding a bus—before he broke.

He curled up in his nest of blankets, hugged his knees to his chest, and fought the ache building in the hollows of his eyes and the pits of his nose and the bottom of his chest until he couldn't anymore. Until the bubble swelling inside him was so big it would rip him apart from the inside out, and he burst, spilling it out in sobs that felt like an engine turning over and refusing to start, hitching and rattling and jerking in his chest. He pressed his face against his thighs and struggled to breathe, but he could hardly manage to gasp a single draught of air past the knot in his throat.

He couldn't do this. Not like this. He'd been more honest with Grey than he had with anyone his entire life, and it felt more vulnerable than being naked, skin to skin. Even when he loved Jake, loved Michael, loved Arturo . . . it had been through the lie. They'd never known what he was. Never seen *him*. They'd just seen who he wanted to be, his illusion of normal. He'd tried, as much as he could to be himself with them, but he wondered now if they'd loved a farce. If they'd loved what they wanted him to be for them—always for them, never for himself. If they'd loved the way he'd laughed and blushed and teased, the sweet things and the softness, little knowing that underneath it was something only Grey could see:

A broken, bitter, lonely monster, who couldn't pretend to be whole anymore.

If he ever had been to start with. Maybe that was why, in the end . . . they'd always stopped seeing him. He'd known every time when the point of no return came. When he became a shadow in their lives, second to their true love, forgotten for the beauty he gave them that was *from* him but never *about* him. Sometimes he wondered if they'd ever even loved him at all, or if he'd just been part and parcel of the euphoria of creative passion.

What *was* he? Why was he like this?

He swallowed hard and pulled the blankets from over his head, reaching for the recorder on his cluttered desk. Gulping around his sniffles, he hit the Record button and tried to make himself talk, struggling with the words when he could hardly breathe around the weight crushing down on his chest.

"There's a man," he said, scrubbing at his nose, his eyes. "Grey. Grey Jean-Marcelin. I . . . I need to say his name in case anyone ever hears this. Because I want someone other than me to know what he did. And what I did. Because it matters. *He* matters. He's . . . he's beautiful inside. So fucking beautiful, all these things he puts out on the canvas . . . There are worlds inside him, worlds I've never seen, worlds I can't imagine, and he wants to snuff them all out."

He shuddered, clutching at his chest. "He tried to kill himself. He came in on my shift the other night with a channel cut down the side of his skull from a shotgun blast. He still wants to die. And I'm helping him. I shouldn't feel guilty when it's what he wants, but I do. I feel selfish. Like I'm preying on him by giving him what he wants, when I don't even know why he wants it. I don't understand it. I don't know if I *can* when I want so much to live that I . . . I do the things I do. But I don't have to understand it, I suppose. It's his choice."

He pressed his face into his palm, dragging the heel of his hand against his wet, sticky cheeks. "I hardly know anything about him except that he makes beautiful art and he sees through me like I'm made of glass. And he . . . he made me see something I've been refusing to look at." He bit down on the inside of his cheek. "I . . . I think I'm leanan sidhe. How, I don't know. I thought . . . I looked at the idea. A long time ago. At least a hundred years, but . . . every story was a woman. *Every. One.* A woman who became a powerful faerie spirit to take revenge on men for the man who destroyed her in her mortal life. I looked and looked and *looked* but couldn't find one story of a male leanan sidhe. And I was stupid and thought because I'm a man, I couldn't be. Everything else fit. It all added up, but because of one stupid assumption, one technicality, I threw it out the window."

Pausing, he laughed, raspy and scraping his throat. "No." He *thunked* his head back against the edge of the papasan chair, looking up at the ceiling. God, he was a fool. A blind fool with his head in the sand. "I ignored it because I didn't want a definitive answer. As long as someone *else* didn't say it, it wasn't real. Just speculation. All this time I've been searching, but I didn't actually want to know. Knowing raises too many more questions, and makes it even harder when I don't know if they'll ever be answered."

He smiled to himself, lips aching as much as the too-hard throb of his heart. No, it wasn't supposed to be like this—one night with Grey ripping off the bandage on a wound that had never healed, forcing Saint to look at the infection he'd been willfully ignoring, pretending as much with himself as with anyone else. Peter Pan syndrome, acting as if, as long as he didn't acknowledge it, nothing would change and he would never, ever have to grow up into the harshness of his own reality.

The problem with never growing old was never having to grow up.

"But like he said . . . it's the twenty-first century. I suppose I need to bloody well let go of my nineteenth-century ideas about gender." He sighed. His breaths shuddered. He was so *cold*. "All I want to know is what he asked me."

He almost couldn't stand to ask. Almost couldn't stand to wonder, when it made him feel so small, so lost, so forgotten. So unwanted.

But he had to know:

"If I'm leanan sidhe . . . who made me this way?"

He lifted the recorder, holding it over his head, looking up past it to the spangles of stars thrown on the ceiling from the cutout lamps scattered all over the room. The numbers ticked by, waiting for him. For a moment they wavered, his vision blurring dizzily, black sparks appearing around the edges. It always happened this way, and talking wouldn't help it. Wouldn't change it. He didn't know what else to say. This still felt so pointless, so self-indulgent, and it wasn't helping him remember anything. It felt more like . . . putting together a puzzle.

One of those puzzles made up of little toothpick slivers of wood that were supposed to form complex buildings and cityscapes, but Saint barely had enough pieces to put together a little shanty—even if he was trying desperately to collect more.

"I'm just collating data, as they say." He laughed; it cut the inside of his throat with whispers. "*Firefly*. Loved that show. Reminded me of *Buck Rogers*. God, I remember when that was still a new thing. I've . . . watched these people live and die, build and grow and tear it all down again. From puppet shows to IMAX. From covered wagons to rechargeable electric cars. From Morse code telegraphs to high-speed internet. I've seen everything, but I've never seen *myself*. Or anyone like me. I don't know anything about leanan sidhe. They're not a thing of this modern Western world. I remember reading things in books on mythology, here and there . . . weaknesses. How to ward against the fae with charms and spells, bits of wood and metal. Certain elements. I've always thought those random feelings of weakness were a sign that I was beginning to fade again, but I wonder if sometimes it was contact with certain elements. Testing could prove or disprove it. I can try. I just . . . It frightens me. It could hurt. Or it could be wrong, and then what? What happens if I'm not leanan sidhe, and I'm left with no answers yet again? I don't know. I just . . . don't know."

He let the recorder drop, closed his eyes again, and tried not to think of rough, dark-skinned hands and the soft, curious gleam of deep-set eyes.

"I just know I don't want to do it alone."

✳ 16 ✳

In the shadows of his apartment, Grey lit his candles and sparked off a stick of incense and knelt before the veve with the scents of teakwood rising and coiling thickly around him, the waft of smoke like fur inside his nose. He traced the patterns he knew by heart, then pressed his hand over his chest and listened to the *thump-thump-thump* that belonged to her and her alone, sworn in such a way that for the longest time, he'd thought he could never give it away to someone else.

"Tell me, Erzulie," he whispered, and watched the flames flicker and dance like silent voices. "What should I do? Is this right? Is *he* right?"

But the loa did not answer, and he wondered if she had already left him, abandoning the useless vessel of his flesh.

⋵ 17 ⋷

Picking up his life and going to work the next night felt anticlimactic. Ridiculous, almost. It was a night of chasing frat keggers, and people were drinking too much and choking on their own vomit and giving themselves alcohol poisoning—when they weren't falling off balconies because they were so very convinced Jägerbombs and vodka shots made them invulnerable to the effects of human stupidity.

Saint didn't know why he was so worried about killing humans, when they were so fucking dead set on killing themselves.

He closed his eyes. *Killing themselves. Ha. Ha. You're so funny, Saint.*

Let's pretend you aren't worried that you haven't heard from him. Not like you left a callback number, handy suicide specialist on call, but . . .

He should be relieved. Grey had realized how terrible this was and backed out. Maybe he'd even decided he wanted to live, and run far and fast in the opposite direction. Good. *Good.* He should stay far away from Saint. Maybe it was time to let go. Die. If his only hope was falling in love, he was fucked anyway.

Who would love something as broken and damaged and bitter as him?

And why did the idea of never seeing Grey again hurt like fucking hell?

"Hey. Earth to Xav."

Nuo flicked his arm. He ignored her and just pulled his jacket closer around himself, gripping the cloth tight so she wouldn't see how his fingers shook. He shouldn't be this tired, though he'd pulled a long shift tonight; they were always scheduled extra hours on Football

Fridays, but at nearly 4 a.m. things had calmed, the emergency room just a quiet tableau of waiting, the calls coming fewer and farther between. He leaned against the ambulance door, soaking in the summer heat, while Nuo sat on the hood and smoked a cigarette and muttered about which one of the doctors would be enough of an asshole to step out of the OR just long enough to report her for smoking on shift.

"*Xav.*" She swung her legs and knocked the toe of her sneaker into his thigh. He sighed, looking up at her. "Hey. You okay? You look sick."

"I'm fine. Just a little cold."

She snorted. "It's ninety-eight out. In the shade."

"It's night. Everything is shade."

"Don't deflect, Xav."

"That's what I'm best at."

She let it lie for a few minutes, pulling at her cigarette in deep draughts and blowing out bitter-smelling clouds. She usually left him alone about things, but he had a feeling she wouldn't this time. He'd known Nuo ever since he decided it was safe to slip his way back into society for a while—when he couldn't stand the loneliness anymore, cooped up in his little tower room hidden out in the hills and the trees and the dripping Spanish moss. She'd been in his EMT certification class. Nervous as hell, clicking a pen in and out, cursing under her breath, pacing outside the classroom while they waited for the first session to open. She'd stepped on his foot. He'd called her a manky git. They'd been friends ever since, but there was always a wall there and he knew damned well it was his fault, and he didn't blame her for having too much self-respect to keep poking and prodding at him when all he did was shut her out.

He was the kind of friend you bitched about work with, maybe had a beer with after-hours now and then. He wasn't the kind of friend anyone trusted with things.

He couldn't be trusted with anything at all.

Nuo held her peace until she'd finished her cigarette, and flicked it to send it arcing to the other side of the roundabout, leaving a smoldering trail of smoke. "Putting on the jaded act again?"

He shrugged. "Who says it's an act?"

"You know, cynical people aren't cynical because they don't feel anything." She leaned back on her hands and swung her legs, kicking her heels against the front tire. "They're cynical because they feel too much, and keep getting hurt for it."

"*Hn.*"

"Yeah, you just keep grunting at me." She grinned and hopped down from the hood. "You're just mad 'cause I'm right. C'mon." She thumped his shoulder. "Help me get Black Betty here put away. It's time to go home."

"I still don't get why you call it that."

"Because you're a Luddite who doesn't spend enough time on the internet."

"Shut up. I have a smartphone."

"You have a Nokia. They could put that thing on display in the Smithsonian."

He just grunted again, but pulled the driver's side door open—then paused as headlights swept the roundabout, turning in. He lifted his head, squinting at the approaching vehicle, but the high beams blinded him until they shut off.

And revealed Grey's battered, broken pickup truck.

Saint froze. His blood crystallized and threatened to shatter with the wild beat of his heart. What was Grey doing here? Had he changed his mind? Or worse—hadn't he? Fuck . . . *fuck*, why did it make Saint's toes curl and his skin prickle to see the man when he knew what it would lead to?

And why couldn't he tear his gaze from the easy, graceful roll of his shoulders or the fluidity of his body as Grey slid out of the truck and strode closer?

Nuo smacked his arm. "Xav?" She leaned into him, whispering in his ear. "Why is the suicidal hot artist guy here *again*?"

"I don't know."

"Is he here for you?"

"I don't *know*."

Grey drifted to a halt a few feet away, glancing from Saint to Nuo, before meeting Saint's eyes with a small, almost rueful smile.

"Hi."

Saint stared at him and tried to ignore the tremor of his knees, the tingle in his palms. "What are you doing here?"

"We're supposed to be having a relationship. I'd like to take you on a date."

For a half a second, Saint was caught in a tug of war between the sweet, light feeling fizzing in his chest and the heavier guilt plunging to the bottom of his stomach.

Then Nuo elbowed him.

Hard.

He winced, hissing through his teeth—but refused to look at her or acknowledge the dull red knot of pain blooming in his ribs, keeping his gaze on Grey and that oddly earnest look on his face, waiting and hopeful. "At four o'clock in the morning?"

"Your snooty coffee shop isn't the only place open all night." Grey spread his hands. "I'm an artist. I don't sleep like a normal daywalker. Or at all. I know every all-night place in Savannah." He grinned—a startling thing, white and inviting against the dark heat of his lips, creasing his eyes into simmering candle flames of so very *human* warmth. "I also know there's nothing that tastes better than IHOP coffee at 4 a.m."

"IHOP." Saint arched a brow. "You're taking me for pancakes on our first date."

"Can you think of anything better?"

He scowled. "Hn."

"Xav?" Nuo asked.

"What."

"You're dating Grey Jean-Marcelin. *The* Grey."

"I don't know."

She huffed. "Stop saying that!"

Grey fixed him with a pointed look, and Saint's face heated, uncomfortable and dizzying and burning his cheeks.

"Are we dating, *Xav*?"

God damn it. With a growl, he turned his back on those— those—they weren't fucking coyote eyes, they were *puppy* eyes, and they weren't going to work on him. "I need to put the ambulance in its bay."

"I'll take care of it!" Nuo chirped, and he glared at her.

"Stop being helpful."

"C'mon." Grey's fingers brushed his arm. "We need to talk."

That's exactly why I don't want to go.

He looked back reluctantly. If he went, he knew exactly what Grey would want to talk about. This *agreement* between them. This agreement he never should have brought up, never should have proposed. Worst idea of his life, and after over two hundred years of mistakes and willful denial, that was saying a lot.

"I will kick you in your skinny butt if you don't go," Nuo said. "For fuck's sake, it's free pancakes."

Grey laughed, a silky rumble like flowing molasses. "Your friend has a point. Who would turn down free pancakes?"

"Stop ganging up on me!"

Nuo grinned. "You're so cute when you're pissy." She offered Grey her hand. "His friend's name is Nuo, by the way. I took your blood draw in the ambulance."

Grey flicked a glance over her, then caught her hand and squeezed. "Thank you. I think. Not exactly a fan of needles."

"But you're a fan of living, right?" Nuo asked.

The stricken expression that crossed Grey's face told Saint everything he needed to know. Fuck. *Fuck.* He pushed away from the ambulance door, shrugging out of his jacket.

"I'll go," he said quickly. Anything to save Grey from having to answer that question when he looked like he'd crack if he tried. Nuo's frown was confused, but Saint ignored her, just taking Grey's hand and pulling him firmly toward his truck. "Come on."

✳ 18 ✳

But you're a fan of living, right?

He should have expected a question like that. It was the kind of question normal people asked, because normal people assumed if you weren't in the bin after a failed suicide attempt, then whatever had gotten turned sideways in your head must have tilted right again, phew, narrow miss, aren't we glad *that* didn't happen?

XEN SANDERS

Except he wasn't. He wasn't glad, and he was a horrible liar. He still didn't know how the hospital shrink had given her stamp of approval and kicked him out, and he suspected it had more to do with understaffing and less to do with his ability to fake a stable mental state.

He barely felt Saint dragging him toward his truck, barely felt the warm, slim fingers in his, barely was aware of the girl—Nuo— watching them with wide, confused eyes. He just heard that question circling over and over again, driving home exactly what he was *doing*. Panic sucked the breath from his lungs; he took several wheezing breaths, stumbling.

Saint whirled back, catching him as he pitched forward, arms sliding around him. "What is it? What's wrong?"

Grey clutched at Saint's shoulders, shaking his head until his vision cleared. "Nothing. N-nothing, I—"

His throat constricted. He nearly gagged trying to get the words out. Saint slipped his arm behind his back and guided him to lean against the hood of the truck, resting hard on his elbows with the rusty paint scraping his forearms.

"Breathe," he said, that lyrical accent soft, soothing. "Count them. In. Out. One. Two. In. Out. Three. Four."

He closed his eyes and listened to that low voice counting, that warmth against him. "In. Out. Five. Six. In. Out. Seven. Eight." As he had last night, Saint pressed against his back, the gentle heat of his body comforting and steady. He clung to that memory, to the calm it brought, to the flush of something exhilarating and nervous it roused inside him, while he tried to calm his breaths and force them in and out, silently counting along in time with that voice guiding him out of the dark.

"Everything okay?" Nuo called.

"He's fine," Saint answered. His fingers stroked slow circles against Grey's stomach, leaving bursts of tingling fire in their wake. "Just a panic attack."

"You sure?"

"Yes."

The tightness in his chest eased. Still counting his breaths in his head, measured and careful, Grey opened his eyes and twisted in

64

Saint's arms to meet his gaze. Those strange eyes looked up at him, shadowed by the veil of sooty lashes, dark with concern. Did Saint actually *care* for him?

How could he, when they knew next to nothing about each other?

"What happened?" Saint murmured.

Grey only shook his head. He couldn't answer that. Not with that girl hovering close by, all curious ears and questioning eyes. "Let's just go. And . . ." He hesitated, struggling. "Thank you."

Saint looked as if he might protest, then nodded, pulling away. But he barely made it three steps, his fingers grasping the handle of the truck door, before his legs buckled and he sagged with a low moan. Grey rushed to catch him, wrapping his arms around Saint's waist from behind, pulling him back against his body. Saint stiffened, not even breathing, like holding frozen flame in his arms.

Let go, Grey told himself. *Let go.* Bondye, they made one hell of a pair, both wobbling about everywhere and one step from falling over. He didn't like those dark circles under Saint's eyes, the ashen pallor adding blue undertones to his already pale skin. But he should damned well let him go, instead of standing here in public like an idiot with his arms slowly tightening around him. He wanted to envelop him, protect him, and for just a moment he caught himself leaning lower, the tip of his nose brushing dark, cool hair.

"You okay?" he asked softly.

Saint made a choked sound, flinching. "I'm fine." He shrugged out of Grey's grip, ripping away almost violently; Grey let his arms fall, stepping back, as Saint tossed him a slit-eyed look and jerked the truck's door open. "Just fine."

He climbed inside, flung himself down against the passenger seat, folded his arms over his chest, and glared mutinously at Grey through the windshield. Grey couldn't help a faint smile, even as hurt knotted deep in his chest. Stubborn thing. Worse than a cat.

You'll help me, but won't let me help you.

Nuo tilted her head. "Um."

Grey glanced back at her and raised a hand. "Good night, miss."

"I—um—sure. Good night."

Grey could only imagine the grilling Saint would get later. But later wasn't now, and for now he rounded to the driver's side of the truck, let himself in, and started the engine. Saint transferred that fierce scowl from Grey to the window; Grey lingered on him for a few moments, then sighed, jacked the truck into gear, and eased it around the ambulance, around the curve of the roundabout, and into the street.

"You're not really fine, are you." He glanced at Saint. "You're getting weak. It hasn't really taken."

Saint slouched in the seat, stuffing himself forcefully down against the ragged upholstery. "What did you want to talk about?"

"Do you really need to ask me that?"

"No. I don't." Saint's leg jittered restlessly, counting *thud-rap-rap, thud-rap-rap* with his knee against the underside of the glove box. "So we're doing this, then."

Are we?

Was Grey suddenly afraid of death, now that he'd reached for Bawon Samedi's hand and fallen short?

He shrugged as neutrally as he could. "If you still want to."

"If I don't, you'll find another way, won't you?"

"Probably," he admitted, even if he was afraid to ask himself the real answer. Afraid to look head-on at that terrible knot of doubt beginning to coil inside him. He stole another glance away from the road and at Saint. "It feels like I'm using you, when you put it that way."

"I'm used to it."

"You shouldn't be." He frowned. "Didn't the others love you? Isn't that how it works?"

Saint looked at his lap, curling his fingers in the edges of his shirt. It was a thin, black, ribbed shirt tonight, sleeveless, those designs down his arms bared in their stark, livid shadow-light; by night they seemed alive, whispering stories in the shapes of a thousand myths. One incisor worried at Saint's lower lip, and for a moment Grey was caught: those teeth were subtly too long, strange, their shape wrong. Some people had naturally pointed incisors, but Saint's were just *off* enough to make Grey look away from the road for a few moments too many.

Was that the way of things when someone wasn't human, then?

The oncoming flash of headlights forced him to jerk his gaze back to the highway, steadying the truck's drift quickly and easing back into the lane in time to pass a drunkenly speeding black sedan that might just be Nuo's problem sooner rather than later. Saint still hadn't answered. Grey couldn't bring himself to push him. Not when he could feel the presence of so many dead like ghosts haunting the cab of the truck, this shadow between them, wordless and yet screaming into the silence.

"I don't know anymore," Saint finally said, faint, barely more than a whisper. "I thought they did. But if I'm honest with myself, if I stop pretending everything will be all right if I just *love* them enough . . . I don't know if they loved me, or if I was just part of the intensity of emotion that comes with what I do to them. Passion is passion, after all. They mostly forgot me, once it took hold. It was all about their art. I suppose sometimes . . . sometimes they remembered I was still there." He let out a bitter snort. "When I put it that way . . . I don't think it was *me* they loved at all."

"That doesn't seem right."

"I was killing them. There was nothing right about that situation." Saint laughed, a hitching gasp of sound, and tilted his head back against the seat. "There's nothing right about *this* situation."

Grey couldn't stand it. That quiet pain, that horrible breaking in Saint's voice. He pulled one hand off the wheel and offered it to Saint, just . . . asking. He wasn't going to take, when it felt like so many others had already taken from Saint, even if they'd paid with their lives. But he wanted to do something, *anything* to, just this once, make it easier on this withdrawn, sullen, beautiful man who made himself such a harsh tangle of thorns, but only kept stabbing himself every time he tried to stab someone else.

"I don't want to forget you're here," Grey said. "Please."

Saint eyed his hand and leaned away. "Why not?"

"I just . . . don't." He shook his head. "Hasn't anyone ever wanted you for yourself, not what you can do for them?"

"I . . ." Saint made that awful sound again, that one he'd made outside the truck, like two hundred years of heartbreak in one tiny whimper. He lifted his hand, started to reach for Grey's. "I don't know."

"Do you want someone to?"

Saint jerked back, clutching his hand against his chest as if that moment of near-contact had stung; as if Grey were poison, full of venom, full of hurt. His glare cut deep, as Grey let his hand fall.

"If I did, you wouldn't exactly be the one, would you?" Saint said, then shifted in the seat to curl on his side, giving Grey nothing but his back.

Grey sighed, gripping the steering wheel again. Such a prickly thing. So defensive. So angry.

So why did it just make Grey want to find the bleeding heart underneath his wall of thorns?

✳⚬ 19 ⚬✳

Silence was the order of the evening on the rest of the drive. Grey was starting to think they were made for tense silences: Saint pretending he wasn't there, Grey driving faster as if he could outrun the thoughts chasing him. He hadn't been afraid in that moment he'd felt everything go black, the pain a dull throb of fire raked down the side of his skull, his blood a sticky pool spreading beneath him with a warmth that was almost comforting, like the embrace of amniotic fluid taking him back to the darkness where he'd first been born. He'd felt nothing but peace, then. Peace, acceptance, a hope he'd bleed out before anyone found him. That night he'd had nothing to lose, and no reason to be afraid.

Did the tremor of his heart, the doubt, the questions, mean he had something to lose now? Was that why he'd felt that moment of wrenching, terrible panic and fear?

He stole a glance at Saint, watching how the oncoming headlights swept over his skin in alternating bands of ivory and gold, occasionally catching in his eyes and lighting them up like a rose-colored dawn before fading into twilight again. At least the other man had relaxed, uncurling from his defensive ball and sinking down to face forward again, even if his gaze focused anywhere but on Grey. But for a half second he caught Saint watching him from the corner of his eye, just a quick, darting glance before he huffed and looked away with a scowl. Grey's lips quirked.

For an inhuman black widow, sometimes Saint was disgustingly cute.

The sign for the IHOP flashed up ahead: blue, red, and white against the night. Grey switched lanes and then pulled into the lot. He expected a dirty look when he got out to open the door for Saint, and he wasn't disappointed.

"Why do you do that?" Saint asked.

"Because I want to. Do I need another reason?"

"I'm not a damsel, and I'm not in distress."

"I don't think a closed door is enough of a crisis to put anyone in distress." Grey chuckled, pocketed his keys, and strode toward the restaurant. "Inside. Free pancakes."

"You really are going to make me hate you if you keep trying to be clever."

"Trying?"

"*Trying.*"

Grey laughed and, just to be an ass, held the restaurant door too. He was rewarded by another fierce, petulant glare before Saint stormed past him and inside. His pout held until the waitress seated them and left their menus. Grey chose to keep his silence until they'd ordered; sitting across from each other like this with their knees brushing and the table bringing them so close, he didn't quite trust Saint not to take advantage and kick him where it would hurt the most if he said the wrong thing.

But once the waiter had taken their menus and left a carafe of coffee, Grey risked opening his mouth. "It won't kill you to look at me, you know."

Saint propped his chin in his hand and glared out the window to the parking lot. "You don't know that. It might. Maybe leanan sidhe are allergic to smart-ass jerks."

"Am I really such a jerk?"

"*Hn.*"

"So expressive." Grey chuckled and poured both their cups full, shaking out a few creamers and a couple of sugar packets into his own before nudging the little condiment island toward Saint. "So you're definitely a leanan sidhe now?"

"Don't say it like that. It sounds like you don't believe me. You're the one who said it."

"I didn't say I didn't believe you. You were the one who didn't like the idea."

Saint scrunched his nose and stuck his tongue out, reaching for the sugar packets and counting out eight-nine-ten-*eleven* before beginning to rip them open and dump them in. "I don't know. It makes sense. I mean, a lot of things have made sense, though—and I think I've been afraid to settle on just one, only to end up being wrong. There are legends of lamiae and incubi and . . . so many other things, and so many could fit for one reason or another. All of them? Some kind of sexual being who preys on the energy of men, filling them with a fever of passion for one thing or another, burning them out, draining them dry." He shrugged. "If anything, it means human mythology reflects a complete and absolute terror of sex. And women, but mostly just sex in general."

"You're not a woman. And I'm not afraid of sex."

"That is an absolutely terrible pickup line."

Grey grinned. "I wasn't offering sex with *you*."

Saint blinked; color climbed up his cheeks like creeping vines, and if Grey hadn't been offering sex before, he'd be damned well tempted now when that blush brought out everything delicate and sweet in that fragile face, everything warm and vulnerable—and he wanted to cradle those lovely features in his palms and feel that heat soak into his skin.

"Seriously," Saint muttered. "This doesn't fucking work if I hate you."

"I'll behave." But Bondye, he didn't want to. "So. Leanan sidhe. Why does it make more sense?"

Another glower. Saint growled something under his breath. "Mostly because . . . they were all creative types. All of them. Jake was an author. Philippe was a graffiti artist. Arturo, a cellist. Dorian was a theater performer back in the . . ." He frowned. His eyes unfocused, misting. ". . . God, I can't remember. I *can't*. I know it was in the late eighteen hundreds, I just . . ." He shook his head. "The years kind of . . . *blend*, after a while. I spend so much time alone . . ."

"You'd have to, wouldn't you?" Grey asked. He was afraid to pry, but fuck if he didn't want to know more. More about this fascinating creature and what he might be; more about this beautiful thing his life would burn to fuel. "To keep from being discovered."

Saint hugged his arms to himself, rubbing at his biceps. "I can only stay for a few years here and there. Ten to fifteen at most, before people start to notice things. Then . . . a decade, two, hiding away."

"But you stay in Savannah?"

"Near. I get . . . I don't know how to explain it. Sick, if I leave too long. As sick as if my time was running out again. So there's this house, out in the hills . . ."

"Your home?"

Saint nodded mutely, fixing his gaze on the table. Grey reached out to touch the peak of his chin, tracing the soft skin.

"Will you show me one day? Let me see?"

"I . . ." Saint licked his lips and darted a glance at him from beneath his lashes. "If I do, I . . . I need your help."

"I thought that was already established."

"No." Oddly muted, an almost childish sound. He shook his head. "There may be a way to test if I really am. Leanan sidhe, I mean. Things that should hurt me, or make me weak. I want to try, but . . . but . . ."

"But you don't want to do it alone," Grey finished. Saint nodded, jerking his gaze away again, pulling back from his touch, and Grey smiled. "Of course."

"You mean that?"

"Why wouldn't I?"

Saint curled one hand against his chest, rubbing as if trying to ease the pain of a wound. "I . . . I don't . . ."

He broke off as the waiter returned with their plates, sliding a steaming Denver omelet in front of Grey and a stack of sweet-smelling pecan pancakes in front of Saint, almost ludicrous with their comical little pat of butter standing on top. Saint murmured something polite under his breath, while Grey flashed a smile and waved the waiter off. He didn't know how to ask what Saint had been about to say . . . and so he didn't.

"I . . . I don't . . ." what?

Instead he unrolled his fork and knife from the napkin and offered a lame "Bon appétit"—then watched with skeptical amazement as Saint picked up one of the syrup carafes and upended it above his plate, dumping nearly the entire thing over the pancakes until the syrup puddled and threatened to overflow the edges of the plate. Grey arched a brow and picked up another carafe, offering it without a word.

Saint blinked at it quizzically, tilting his head, then darted Grey a confused glance. "Oh—no, I don't need any more."

"You sure? I think there's a small island of pancake above sea level."

"Shut it."

Grey only *looked* at him, biting back a grin. Saint blinked again, then glared to one side.

Then he laughed.

A thrumming vibrato like the last fading quivers of a piano's strings after a ringing, stirring crash of notes, and Grey's eyes lidded with pleasure to hear it. Just that simple laugh lit Saint's gaze until sunset became the dawn, and his lips enticed, pursing into a little raspberry as he made a face at Grey.

"I've got a sweet tooth, all right?" He reached for his fork—then faltered, glancing back at Grey, eyes widening slightly. "What? Why are you staring at me like that?"

"That's the first time I've heard you laugh. I didn't think you were capable."

He immediately wished he'd said nothing when that laughter, that smile, vanished. Saint lowered his gaze to his plate. "We haven't exactly discussed things worth laughing over."

"Truth," Grey acknowledged, and picked up his own fork—but not without one last glance at the lovely creature currently pushing the sodden mush of pancakes around his plate. "Am I making you uncomfortable?"

"You keep *looking* at me."

"Has no one ever looked at you before?"

"No one who can see what I am."

"*What.* Not *who.*" Sudden frustration pushed a growl up Grey's throat. "You talk about yourself like you're a *thing.* I don't like it."

Saint lifted his head sharply, staring at him again. It was hard to believe he was so old, Grey thought, when he so often gazed at him with the innocent, confused surprise of a wounded child.

"Are . . . Grey, are you treating this like something serious?"

"Shouldn't I?" *Don't touch him. Don't.* When he wasn't playing seductive, Saint was like a small, skittish animal, and Grey didn't want to spook him away. He forced himself to focus on his omelet, though the idea of eating it—all that grease and densely layered cheese and gristly meat—was much less appealing than it had been when he ordered. "It's a business arrangement. I get that. An exchange of the strangest currency ever. The most Faustian bargain on earth. But . . . Bondye, Saint. You don't want me to love you, but can't I at least like you while we're doing this together?"

Saint scowled and stuffed a bite of pancake into his mouth. "There's nothing to like about me."

"You don't get to tell me what I do or do not like." He reached out and brushed his thumb against a drip of honey-brown pouring from the corner of Saint's lips, smiling to himself. "And right now I like a pretty, fey man who happens to have syrup dripping down his chin."

He was rewarded by that flush that bewitched him so much, and Saint's flustered mumble as he wiped at his mouth, then checked his fingers. His brows knit before he made an exasperated noise that sounded suspiciously like a repressed laugh.

"Oh, just eat the fucking omelet you bullied me into coming here for."

Grey grinned. He couldn't help it. He couldn't remember the last time he'd smiled this much, and he leaned over the table in an awkward attempt at a bow.

"As my fae lord commands."

"Grey?"

"Yes?"

"Shut. Up."

With a laugh, Grey cut off a segment of his omelet and stuffed it into his mouth.

Dying, he thought, had never felt quite so good.

✳ 20 ✳

Saint had never been overly fond of Shakespeare. He'd read the plays sometime in the early nineteen hundreds, when he'd been going stir-crazy in his little prison of a tower. He'd read thousands of books for that reason. Taken up a million hobbies, abandoned just as many. Wandered the hills, seen only as a ghost by the occasional hunter or playing child. Stayed up all night doing nothing and learning to understand the value of nothing. But he'd never quite seen the point of a story about star-crossed lovers fated to die.

Why, then, had he walked directly into one?

He tried to ignore Grey as they ate. Tried to ignore everything but the taste of maple syrup and sugar-crusted pecans and deliciously soggy pancake. At least Grey was gracious enough not to *talk*. But every time their knees brushed under the table, every time their hands touched when they reached for the coffeepot at the same time, every time their feet nudged as they shifted, they stopped. Looked.

And Saint always looked away first, because he couldn't stand the intensity of those feral eyes tearing into him, trying to know him. Trying to find that key inside him that would make the gears click together to begin the downward spiral, the machine of his curse grinding Grey toward death.

If it wasn't already. If it wasn't already rumbling in each shuddering beat of Saint's heart, each constriction of his throat when they touched skin to skin and every inch of his body prickled.

You don't want me to love you, but can't I at least like you while we're doing this together?

He didn't understand how Grey could. Would Jake have still loved him if he knew Saint was the reason for his wasting sickness? Would Philippe?

Be honest with yourself. Stop pretending it was you *they ever loved.*

"I'm dishonest," he blurted, breaking the silence, feeling like he was breaking glass. He stared down at his fork, twirling its tip in the puddles of syrup. "I told you I'm not good with the truth. I'm dishonest. I'm a liar. You shouldn't like a liar."

Grey's fork clinked against the plate. In his peripheral vision, Saint saw the base of Grey's coffee cup lift and then fall again, setting down with a soft *thud*. Every second dragged out agonizingly until Grey finally spoke. "It seems like your biggest problem is that you *are* being honest with me."

"Maybe." He gulped, fighting the tightness in his throat to swallow. "It makes me realize how much I lied to everyone else."

"Would knowing have saved them?"

"No, but . . . I could have given them a choice, like I gave you . . ."

"And they wouldn't have believed you." Warm fingers touched under his chin, guiding him to look up, to look at Grey, into that smile that was so understanding it hurt. "Are you really hating yourself for what you have to do to survive?"

"*Yes!*"

"Do you think the cat hates itself when the mouse dies?"

"*They weren't mice!*" He shoved Grey's hand away, his eyes brimming with an abruptness that nearly slapped the breath from him. "They were men. Men I loved. You aren't a mouse. Don't talk about yourself that way. If I'm not a *thing*, then you're not a *mouse*."

"All right," Grey said. "I don't mind being more to you than a mouse."

He recoiled. "That's . . . that's not what I meant . . ."

"No?"

His lips trembled. He was grateful for the waiter interrupting this time, with the check. It let him look away from Grey. Outside, the night was almost moonless, just a sliver of light like someone had taken a penknife to the dark canvas of the sky and cut out a little piece to keep. He stared at it and tried to shut out the sounds of Grey telling the waiter they didn't need anything else, the noise and chatter of people all around them, these *people* with normal lives who never had to worry about anything when they fell in love except for a broken heart. He'd told himself after the first few times that it wasn't any different than when one spouse died before another, but to do it over and over again . . .

"Saint?"

Grey had stood, and now his fingers brushed Saint's shoulder, pulling him back to reality. He risked one look at him from the corner of his eye, then looked away again.

"What?"

"Did you want to stay here longer?"

"You paid?"

"I asked. I paid."

"You didn't have to—"

"You keep telling me that. You need to learn the difference between *have to* and *want to*." Grey offered his arm, crooked and waiting. "I'd like to take you somewhere, if you'll come with me."

No, Saint wanted to say. *No*. Because that offered arm was dangerous. That offered arm was heartbreak waiting to happen, a promise that he could and would fall in love with Grey and hate himself for the way it would have to end. Every time he tried to hold them, and every time they slipped through his fingers like sand through his broken hourglass.

No, he told himself, then tucked his hand into the crook of Grey's arm and stood.

"Sure," he murmured, and loathed the taste of the word on his tongue. "Sure."

✳꞊ 21 ꞊✳

At least this time, the silence in the truck wasn't quite so tense. Saint tucked himself into a ball in the passenger's seat, rested his head against the window, and tried not to fall asleep. Now and then the raggedy truck jounced on a buckle in the pavement and jolted him awake, before he found his eyes growing heavy again. He could blame it on the hectic night at work, but he knew what it really was. The weakness, crawling into his bones and sucking the marrow from him. He pictured it as one of the wild things in Grey's paintings, this thing so inhuman that it should be ugly but was only strange and alien and incomprehensible and beautiful. Neither good nor evil, just like Grey's loa.

It just . . . was what it was.

He looked up when archways of perfectly groomed, cultivated trees closed over them, leading the truck down cobbled roadways like the aisle of a church leading them to the altar. Forsyth Park.

He peeked out the window at the night, watching the moon play peep-bo with the branches and leaves until Grey pulled the truck onto the curb and parked. He flashed Saint a smile and slipped out to hold the door for him again. This time, when Grey offered his arm, Saint slipped his fingers into the crook without question, and let himself—for just a moment, in this quiet dark of night that smelled of mossy green things and wet, crisp dew—lean against the warm curve of the other man's shoulder.

Grey guided him across the pathways, between trees almost as old as Saint himself, surrounded by carefully manicured bushes and flowers that filled the air with a sweet, musty scent. As they broke into the plaza surrounding the great pale stone fountain, Grey slowed, gaze trained up to the sky. Saint tilted his head back—and caught himself watching not the night, but Grey, outlined in deep, richly gleaming brown against dark blue, the stars seeming to trace a path of constellations along the lines of his profile.

"Why the park?" he asked, and Grey looked down at him with a slow smile.

"The fountain," he answered, and pulled away to grip the fence walling off the fountain. His body flexed, tight and powerful, and then he vaulted over, landing lightly on the paving stones on the other side.

Saint laughed, draping his arms along the fence. "Grey! You're not supposed to—"

"Come on."

Grey leaned over the wrought iron, caught him around the waist, and lifted him. He couldn't stop his laughter, rushed from inside him in a breathless gasp, as the world tipped up and sideways, swirling past like a shaken kaleidoscope as Grey swung him across the fence—and spun him around to deposit him right *in* the fountain in water up to his knees, instantly soaking his trousers and clinging them to him in a cold film. The spray from the central font sprinkled down on him in a drizzle, cold droplets pattering into his hair and shoulders. He laughed, clutching at Grey's arms as the other man climbed in with him, the water swirling against their legs in almost musical waves. Saint shivered until Grey's arms slid around his waist, drawing him into the heat of Grey's body, sharp contrast burning between them until he felt every lean line of slinking, agile muscle coiling against him like ropes of silk.

He looked up, meeting stark golden eyes. Grey was such a portrait of contrasts, nearly monochrome save twin bright spots of color, and Saint couldn't resist reaching up to twine his fingers against the back of Grey's neck, fingertips playing against the soft burr of pale, close-cropped hair.

"We aren't supposed to *be* here," he said, biting back another laugh.

"I haven't gotten caught yet. I come here to think, sometimes. I like the quiet of it. It feels like being somewhere that isn't here. Somewhere that isn't anywhere. Like I'm just . . . floating in this place between waking and sleeping, both in this world and out of it."

"*In* the water?"

"In the water." With a chuckle, Grey leaned down, resting his brow to Saint's. So close, his breaths a curling caress that wisped and slithered along Saint's jaw. Sweet, like syrup. Stroking. Tracing an airy fingertip, a phantom tongue, down his throat, until his pulse beat in a single hard leap and he ached to . . . to . . .

He licked his lips. Grey's mouth was too close, tempting cherry-blackberry lushness parted on a tongue that promised gilded things and the taste of darklight fire. He thought Grey would taste of his loa, and the longing to *know* made Saint want to run.

His hands pressed to Grey's chest and he twisted, breaking that hold. Grey's arms fell, and Saint turned from that look of disappointment, fixing his gaze upon the spray tinkling into the fountain's pool.

"You're stupid," he said breathlessly.

"I just might be." Grey moved to stand next to him, tilting his head back to watch the fountain. He laced his hands behind his back. "Do you remember anywhere before Savannah?"

"No. Nowhere. I've lived here since . . . since before this park even existed." He reached out and let the cold spray patter down over his fingertips, striking in little stinging kisses. "I left once, though."

"Where?"

"China. In the late nineteen hundreds. Nineteen ninety . . . four, I think? Maybe ninety-five."

"Bondye." Grey laughed a bit shakily. "I wasn't even in high school by then. What was in China?"

"I wanted to see the Walled City in Kowloon before it was torn down." He shrugged. "But until then . . . I didn't travel much. I'm tied to Savannah. I only lasted a week in China before I had to come back. It's like a compulsion, pulling the strings of my life tight."

"Did you ever come here? To this park?"

"Not often. This was privately owned land for a very long time, before it was donated for the park. Street urchins and trespassers shot on sight."

"Street urchin. It suits you. Is that what you were, back then?"

"For a while."

Saint smiled to himself, watching his hand as he turned it left to right, sending the fountain spray sheeting in one direction or another. But if he unfocused his eyes he could almost see not the fountain, but the land that once stood here: rolling green and untouched trees, human lives nothing but glimpses of peaked roofs over the tops of the leaves, and somewhere the baying of hounds and the clatter of hooves signaling the passing of a hunting party through the brush. Such different days, then. Sometimes it felt like a storybook, a thing he'd made up to fill in for his missing memories. Maybe that was the truth of it, he thought. Maybe he was delusional. Maybe he only believed he'd lived as long as he had, and the rest of it was just the dream of a fevered mind.

No. No—he couldn't believe the pain of every life graven on his skin was something he'd *imagined*. Jake didn't deserve to be a figment of his imagination. Remy. Remy, with his pale gray eyes and the sweet spiderwebs of red capillaries turning his eyelids blush, wasn't a *dream*. They were real.

I'm real.

"One day I just . . . woke up in the street," he said. He had to say it, because he had to make it real. Had to tell someone other than an unfeeling tape recorder, someone who'd believe him, the first person to ever know him for what he was. His fingers curled tight and he pressed them over his chest, as if their damp coolness could ease the fire of his heart burning itself to ash. "No injuries. No belongings, not even a scrap of paper in my pockets. No memory, nothing of my own but the clothes on my back. I was in one of the unfinished planned wards of town, but I didn't . . . didn't know where I was. The first word I saw was the half-painted sign on a building under construction. 'Saint.'" He couldn't help but laugh, now, at his whimsy in taking that for his name. "I knew how to read it. I know how to speak English. I understood basic concepts. Math and reading and reasoning. Not to stand in front of a moving carriage. Not to drink lye. The sun rose and set, and the world required money to turn round. When someone told me I was in Georgia, in the year seventeen ninety-six, I understood what that meant."

A dry burn haunted the corners of his eyes, remembering those first moments. The disorientation. The fear. The confusion. The painful, ripping sense of *loneliness*, and the strangest feeling that he'd lost something more than just a name, a few decades of history.

Grey said nothing. Saint wished he would—anything to fill the silence, to take the weight of these words off his shoulders. But there was only Grey's presence, dark and waiting and warm, and Saint shivered, knotting his fingers in the front of his shirt.

"I knew everything except who I was," he finished, fighting his voice to keep it from cracking, his throat dry as crumbling earth. "So I became Saint, because that word was the first memory I had. I made a new me. And I watched Savannah grow around me."

Slowly, long fingers clasped over his own. Gentle. Strong. And it was that gentle strength that pried his hand free from his shirt, coaxing it to open until Grey could envelop it in his. He lifted Saint's hand and clasped it against his chest, until the beat and throb of his body soaked into Saint's palm and his eyes lidded, his breaths catching with pleasure. He could *feel* it: a thin and tenuous crimson thread stretching between them, curling tendrils waiting, waiting to intertwine, flickering in rhythm with Grey's pounding heart.

"When did you first realize you were immortal?" Grey asked softly.

That warmth dashed, snuffed, leaving behind a dark cold as if the stars inside Saint had gone out all at once. He stared up at Grey, who was night against night, dark and forbidding, colored in the same deep blues as his paintings. Saint's heart shriveled. He looked away. He tugged on his hand, but Grey wouldn't let go.

"I . . ." *Say it.* Spit it out. Let Grey judge him for judging *him*, when Saint had once made the same choice. "I tried to kill myself." He heard Grey's sharply indrawn breath, but didn't let it stop him. "After Calen. He was the first. The wasting sickness took him. He . . . he took me in. He made me feel safe when I was completely lost. He made me someone, instead of a paper doll waiting for an identity to clip on." *Calen with his elegant hands and short, blunt nails, the cuff of lace around his wrist, that curl of hair that always fell over one eye.* The tattoo on his shoulder blade, the striking lines of a rearing mad horse made of otherworldly bright flame, burned against his skin. "And then . . . he died. And nothing I could do could save him. I didn't realize it was my fault, then. But I felt so adrift, so lacking in identity without him, that I tried to drown myself in the Savannah River."

He tried to speak clinically, but the taste of dank river water was in his throat, cold and choking off his airways with the memory. "It was . . . an unsettling experience, to feel myself die and not be dead. An unbreathing corpse at the bottom of the river, completely aware but unable to move until I washed up on shore and my body slowly put itself back together." *Feeling flesh crawling, twisting back together, sealing over the holes where the fish had nibbled, water pumping out of his lungs in sour gasps . . .* He shuddered, looking down at the water, flicker-flash of moonlight on ripples like breaking glass. "I've never had the urge to try it again," he whispered. "Dying terrified me more than not knowing who I am."

Grey released his hand, leaving it empty. He waited for the words, the accusations.

How dare you?

The condemnation. The judgment.

You're a hypocrite.

Instead lean, strong arms slid around him, gathering him close against Grey's body. The other man nearly curled around him, resting his chin to the top of Saint's head, enveloping Saint in that warmth he'd felt only as a brushing tendril before. It wrapped him up tight now, swallowed him into Grey, and Saint ached inside as he pressed his cheek against Grey's chest and, for just a moment, let himself hide. Let himself want.

Let himself wish that this time it could be different, and he wasn't meeting Grey only to say goodbye.

"Saint," Grey whispered. "*Saint.*"

"Don't. Please, just . . . just . . ." He swallowed back a hitched noise, and scrubbed at his eyes. "Don't say a word."

He trembled against Grey while the man held him; he told himself he wouldn't cry, he *wasn't* crying, yet every dry, heaving breath felt like a sob without tears. The only sound between them was the rush of their breaths and the rainfall cry of the falling water, splashing over and over into the fountain. Saint held fast to Grey until he could breathe again, until he no longer felt the crushing weight of every year, every life, wrapped around his neck in a strangling noose of guilt and shame. The soothing touch of Grey's fingers, stroking up and down his back, eased that pressure. His lungs felt like a million tiny fists clenched to straining, but finally those fists relaxed to let oxygen slip through their fingers. The quiet of this shouldn't have been so comforting, standing in a cold fountain with Grey's arms around him.

But right now, it was everything.

He stayed until he couldn't stand it. Until the silence became waiting, the park so still, the leaves unmoving, the night holding its breath and wanting something from this moment. Something from this heaviness, this sweetness between them. Something from his tight-clutched heart, something that would unravel its knot to make it bloom, opening up to let Grey inside.

Saint hunched into himself and leaned harder into Grey. "What really happened tonight?"

Grey stirred as if waking from a dream. "Hm?"

"When you panicked."

"I . . ." Grey pulled back, looking down at him. A ghost of something flickered in his eyes, some unspoken question, then vanished. "It hit me. All of this. What we're doing. I'm treating it so glibly, but . . ." His lips worked, soundless, before finally forming words. "It's big. It took me months to work myself up to trying it before. And now?" His fingers curled against Saint's shoulders. "Now I have to choose. It was still a spur-of-the-moment thing, before. For all my thinking and worrying and planning, *doing* it was an instant decision, and I still had that moment to turn back. I don't, now. Once it starts, it doesn't stop. It's out of my control. And doing it that way, it just feels . . . enormous."

Saint closed his eyes and rested his cheek to Grey's chest. "I know. I know it does." His fingers snared in the other man's shirt. "It's all right if you change your mind. It really is."

"If I do . . . what happens to you?"

"It doesn't matter."

"I think it does."

He shook his head, cheek rubbing thin, fine cotton, cool atop the heat of Grey's body. "Don't, Grey. Don't do this for me." His death grip on the shirt relaxed, and he wrapped his arms around Grey's shoulders, holding on to him as if, if he just clung hard enough, he could really convince himself he could keep him this time. Convince himself that Grey wasn't sacrificing himself so Saint could live. "I can't pretend to understand why. I can't. Not when I've nearly died once, and it frightens me to face that again. But it needs to be for you. Not me."

Grey sighed. He bent over Saint, their cheeks brushing, skin to warm, tantalizing skin. "What if doing this for you *is* for me?"

"I don't . . ." Saint's throat tightened. "I don't know how to make sense of that."

Rough, heated fingers cradled his face, coaxed him to look up. He didn't want to. He didn't want to meet Grey's eyes and see that fatalistic acceptance, that perfect calm, serene and beautiful. But he couldn't avoid it, and his heart broke as Grey stroked his hair back from his brow and smiled.

"You don't have to." Yellow eyes flicked down, lingered on Saint's lips until they tingled with the promise of a perfect, burning touch. "I think I'll kiss you now."

Saint's lips parted. To question, to protest—he would never know when he never had the chance. Not when Grey's lips stole his, stole *him,* and carried him away with a kiss made up of sighs on silk and the taste of amber. He kissed like sugar, sweet and gritty, and Saint clutched at his arms and leaned into the taste of him and opened his mouth to breathe him in. Gasping warmth crept into him, stroked, teased those sensitive, secret corners of his mouth until he felt Grey *inside* him, caressing somewhere dark and deep that trembled his heart and wrapped him up in inescapable bonds.

This was it. This kiss, this moment, when the stars spun overhead and the earth turned beneath them and the song of the sky was at its quietest. This was when he felt it: the thin bright trembling thread of *Grey*, singing through him like music, shiver-soft notes that whispered of everything he *was*. Everything Saint could love about him, waiting to tangle and touch and melt into one.

He whimpered, pressed into Grey, told himself he wouldn't take hold of that bright thread, and yet it was already knotted around him, binding him into heat and the slow, dark fire of long, strong fingers weaving into his hair, teeth teasing and nibbling his lips to tingling-sweet sensitivity, lean sinew burning against him. Fine tremors rippled over his skin, and he surrendered a battle already lost, letting himself rise high on the dizzying, twisting thing coursing through him with every liquid taste of Grey.

I'm sorry, he thought dimly, as their breaths mingled and he gave his gasps into the depths of Grey's mouth. *I'm sorry, so sorry for wanting you . . .*

As if he'd heard him, Grey drew back—slowly, tormenting him with one stolen taste after another, each one softer, drawing just a bit farther away until he was left shivering, looking up at Grey, looking into the dilated, darkened heat of his eyes.

"No more," Grey said, and Saint trembled.

"Why not?"

"Because even if it needs intimacy to work . . . if I'm going to be with you that way, I'm not treating it like a transaction. Not that." He nuzzled the tip of his nose to Saint's. He was so *warm*, until Saint felt like a dead thing next to his wondrous human heat. "I want it to be real. I want it to be you."

With a choked sound, he pulled back, breaking Grey's grip. Oh— oh *god*, he was a horrible person. Because it was happening; he *felt* it happening, this red thing a bloody sun burning in his chest. One kiss. One kiss had made it real, and even if he tried to end this now, tried not to give a damn about Grey . . .

Grey would still die.

He forced a smile, forced himself to try to feel anything but this awful ripping inside. "Is this one of those YA novels about a boy who falls in love with a terminal cancer patient?"

"I'm not your manic pixie dream girl, Saint."

"Then what are you?"

Grey tilted his head with a smile and touched his fingertips to the corners of Saint's mouth. "Maybe you'll figure that out on our next date." With a toss of his head, he waded toward the edge of the fountain. "Come on. I'll take you home."

Saint stared after him, fists clenching helplessly.

Home? But I've never known where home is. Every time I find home . . .

I kill him.

⚜ 22 ⚜

He wasn't supposed to taste so good.

Grey followed the highway out of the city proper, Saint's directions taking him into the deep, low woods where the land started to hump and wrinkle into sloping, graded hills. In the silence between them, all he could hear was the overlapping cadence of breathing, and in it he remembered the way Saint's breaths had rushed out of him and how that lissome body had gone pliant and soft against his own when Grey had twined their tongues and dared to discover just how Saint tasted.

Like everything.

He tasted like *everything*, like the slow-burn beat of blood in his veins, like the drugged addictive bassoon pulse that moved his heart to beat and drove his hands to paint.

And Saint wouldn't even look at him.

Grey let it lie as the winding roadways took them off the paved highway and onto jouncing gravel roads that made the truck groan and rattle, the rusty shocks ready to give up the ghost. One day someone would have to put the old girl out to pasture, but not today. There was history in this truck, in the way the cracked leather seats smelled like pipe tobacco. He pictured his grandfather sitting behind the wheel back when the windshield hadn't been permanently clouded and the dials on the radio weren't falling off. In old photographs, yellowed and stained, his granpé had looked just like him: all stark angles and yellow eyes, and thick soft lips that had whispered poetry even when his grandfather hadn't known how to read or write.

It's in your blood, cheri mwen. Your granpé, he had the passion. He spoke the words like fire. In your paints, in your lines, in your colors, I see his words. His words were what made me love him, but his heart was what made me keep him.

He glanced sidelong at Saint. What did Saint see in his paints and lines and colors that had made him say, *Yes. Yes, I want you?*

By the time he found out, he might well be on his dying breath.

The gravel road turned to dirt, and dirt turned to an overgrown, beaten path with wheel ruts still sunk somewhere under the grass and blooming peonies, guiding the truck like a train on rails. Up ahead, the trees parted on a tall, rickety house, the whitewashed boards faded to milky gray, the shutters hanging off the hinges, the front windows boarded up. Wooden towers had been built to either side, their roofs peaked and conical and shingled in a color that might have once been dark green; hard to tell in the deep of night and sweep of headlights. Vines and moss overgrew the porch, the eaves, threatening to swallow the ancient, leaning plantation home back into the earth. The entire thing looked ready to fall over, and he had a feeling it would have been condemned had anyone in the city even remembered it was out here.

Grey frowned as he eased the truck to a halt. "You live here?"

Saint chuckled wanly. "I do."

"Why?"

"Because no one would expect me to."

"But that can't be safe—"

"It doesn't matter." Saint pushed the door open. "It's mine."

He slammed the truck door closed, then leaned in, resting his arms on the open window. He watched Grey pensively before offering a sweet, wistful smile. "Good night, Grey Jean-Marcelin. Thank you for the pancakes."

"Wait—do you have a car? How are you getting back to the hospital? I could—"

Saint cut him off almost too quickly. "Nuo will pick me up," he said, and pulled back.

"Sure," Grey said, and wondered at the near-physical ache of separation as Saint walked away. "No problem."

He lingered until Saint disappeared into the house, just a glimpse of white and black through the little glass inset in the front door. Then, reluctantly, he pushed the truck into reverse and made his way home.

He'd thought to slip into bed, pull the covers over his head, and try to forget the low heat deep in his belly, a yearning that told him he'd been a fool to let Saint go, to stop that kiss that had consumed him, falling over him like nightfall. It had rocked him, how deeply that one kiss had struck: a crashing thing, shifting his world on its axis, until colors looked different and he felt every sensation so much more keenly, from each droplet of fountain spray on his skin to the fine peach fuzz of Saint's cheeks against his palms.

Was that the power of the leanan sidhe, then? Had Saint compelled him to want him, just by *being*?

With a groan, Grey stretched out on his stomach at the foot of his bed and buried his face against the duvet. This was starting to feel like a hallucination. Maybe he'd really shot himself in the head, and this entire episode was just the last flash of dying synapses as the lights went out. Maybe he'd imagined Saint: this perfect thing, this soft and wounded bird he could cradle in his palms and love in all its broken-winged beauty. His idea of an angel, a loa come to guide him down the path into Bawon Samedi's open arms.

He didn't like that. Thinking this attraction, this hard burst of feeling like a shot of whiskey-burn fire down his gullet, was fake. Artificially induced. *Magic*. That was what it would be, wouldn't it? No. No, magic wasn't . . . It . . .

How could he have faith in the loa and not believe magic existed?

Rolling onto his back, he dragged his hands over his face and stared up at the exposed beams of the ceiling. "Because if it's real," he muttered aloud, "you've just been roofied into falling head over heels."

So what? So what if this feeling was just an illusion? It was getting him what he wanted, in a much less painful way. That was all that mattered.

Right?

He closed his eyes. Too complicated. Too many questions . . . and he sure as hell wasn't anywhere closer to sleep. He hated when he got like this, restless and full of a thousand painful nothings, the darklings chasing themselves in circles inside his head until they wore ruts in his brain. Those ruts were what got him in trouble—because they became permanent, became pathways, and suddenly every new thought diverted down their channels to an end he couldn't avoid. Once those channels had been shallow, and the thoughts could overflow them, spill the banks, run free and rampant.

But now they were a deep and silent river, dragging everything inside him into their depths.

Sighing, he rolled off the bed and crossed the apartment to the mess of canvases and drop cloths scattered everywhere. If he wasn't going to sleep, he might as well do something other than stare at the ceiling and hate himself. Maybe something would come of it; maybe nothing. That was the hell of it. Of this. Sometimes his twisting thoughts fueled his brush, pushed him into a mindless place where he could spill everything out on the canvas.

Sometimes nothing came. Nothing but doubt and self-loathing, holding him back from more than a few sad brushstrokes, so lifeless they might as well be corpses smeared in wet paint.

He set up a fresh canvas, leaning it against the wall, five-by-five and blank white waiting to catch the blood he opened from a vein in his heart. The paints watched him with multicolored eyes, gleaming puddles of color on the palette begging him to dip into their slick coolness, slide his brush and fingers through their wetness, mix and mingle them in torrid swirls. Wasn't he supposed to be inspired? Should he try painting Saint or something?

Hesitantly, he sketched the general outline of a head in pale gray lines of acrylic. Shoulders. This didn't feel right. It felt trite. Even Saint had scoffed and said *Don't bore me*, but he had nothing else right now, and so he traced in arcing dashes marking cheekbones, jawline, the impressions of brows. Only those weren't Saint's brows; Saint's brows were slim and scowling, while these loomed with darker intent. Promising shadows beneath, darkly hollowed, and Grey whirled them in until the outline on the canvas looked more like a skull than a pretty sidhe who stared at him with the eyes of the damned.

And then it took him, and he *understood.*

Dark colors. Dark like the ashes of a fire, dark like a sickle-thin moon glimmering off the surface of slippery-deep, still water. Black on black, night on night, and he bled smoke in his veins and exhaled it from his lungs as he slashed across the canvas and around eyes that burned with the fury of one possessed. He didn't think. Didn't pause to consider color, composition, lighting. Didn't outline, layer, shade, not when he *knew.* The knowing was in his bones, old as the earth, and it spun and pounded and twisted inside him in primal rhythm, caught him up, carried him with the force of the hurricanes that crashed over the islands and swept Haiti in the loa's wrath.

He felt as if a spirit was inside him, using him as a govi for its possession, moving his hand with the dark, wild wishes of the dead. *Something* was inside him, wearing his skin, too much to fit inside one body, threatening to burst out and crushing his lungs until he couldn't breathe. He didn't need to breathe, not when he sucked in life on swirls of color and darkness, not when he burned with this second inner self, this fire, this consumptive and mad thing that roared with a silent voice and trembled pillars of the world with the movements of its slow and ancient shoulders.

This . . . this was electric. His hands shook. Was he high? This starkness, this clarity, this breathless urgency like adrenaline and endorphins cranked up to ten, buzzing and crazed and knotting in the pit of his stomach like sex, and every brushstroke was another thrust into a phantom body . . . they weren't normal. They weren't right, but he couldn't *stop.* It wouldn't let him stop. Not until the sun was well up and across the sky; not until his phone had rung and died a dozen times; not until he painted the last pale violet highlight on the parting of dark-whisper lips.

The brush fell from nerveless fingers that shook with aching cramps, locked in the same position for hours that had felt like days. He stared at the canvas.

Bawon Samedi stared back, his eyes black pits filled with the forgotten dreams of the dead.

White bone painted over skin so black it shone blue and gold, color reflections on a pool of oil. The shadow of the brim of his hat. His leering skeleton grin, grease paint so detailed it still looked fresh and wet even though Grey didn't remember painting it that way, didn't remember the work that went into that sheen of hyperrealism—and yet there it was, stitching a smirk over grim, humorless lips that didn't match that death's head with its broad sickle smile. There was something *real* behind those eyes, something unsettling, as if the demon that was skin-riding Grey had crawled from inside his head to live inside the canvas, and even now looked out at him through Bawon Samedi's livid charcoal eyes.

His hands trembled. His chest hurt. This wasn't his. But it *was*. If the things he painted had been shallow reflections of what he envisioned, pitiful attempts to capture his mind's eye on the canvas... this was a perfect projection plucked from his thoughts and come to life, so true and raw he couldn't stand to look at it.

Not when in those eyes were the dreams of his desire, and a promise.

I am waiting for you, Grey Jean-Marcelin.
Take that pretty white hand, and let him lead you into my world.

✳❧ 23 ❧✳

Saint had barely been awake five minutes before it hit him: heat, washing over and through him with a languid intensity that made him feel like a cat, gasping as he stretched and kneaded against the tangle of his blankets, rolling in the late-afternoon sunlight that poured through the window of his tower room. He arched onto his back, lips parting on a sigh that felt as tangible as flesh passing his lips, caressing over his tongue.

Oh, Saint thought.

Oh, fuck.

He wasn't cold anymore, he realized; if anything he was too hot, and he couldn't quite blame it on drowsing all day in the shifting band of sunlight spilling across the bed. His blood pounded fiercer, stronger, and when he spread his fingers wide the hollows between the tendons were no longer so deep, the shadows no longer so blue. He closed his eyes, his stomach sinking.

Grey was it, then. It was happening already. He'd hoped, in some secret part of him, that it wouldn't take. Even if he died . . . he might be all right with that, as long as Grey found a reason to live.

Wasn't that a fucking catch-22. Caring about Grey enough to want him to live . . .

It was exactly what was killing him.

The sound of a grumbling engine rose from outside. At first he ignored it as he tried to catch his breath, tried to calm that slinking, slow need coiling under his skin and making him burn with a hollowness that craved filling. Sometimes logging trucks passed nearby, or people who got lost on their way to some other backwoods dirt road. But it grew louder, and he opened one eye. He recognized that grumble, distinctive and creaking. With a frown, he tumbled to his knees and peered out the window. Grey's rickety pickup trundled out from beneath the trees, and Saint hated himself for the spark of longing that rose, twining with that blooming heat to twist a heavy, hungry, needy feeling inside him.

What was Grey *doing* here?

Saint spilled off the bed and dumped himself into a pair of jeans, pulling them over his boxers and smoothing his shirt. He made it downstairs just in time to meet Grey as the man mounted the porch steps, a broad grin lighting his face.

"Saint."

"Why—"

Grey caught him around the waist, lifted him, *spun* him; he yelped and clutched Grey's shoulders—only to find himself gathered close against Grey's body. Grey curled around him, burying his face in his shoulder, and embraced Saint with something close to desperation.

"I needed to see you. Saint, it *happened*."

He breathed out shakily and nodded, resting his brow to Grey's throat. "I know."

I just don't understand how you can seem so happy about it.

Drawing back, Grey cupped his cheek, searched his face. "You look better," he murmured. "Healthier."

"For all you know, I just got a good day's sleep."

"It's possible. But unless you drugged me, I doubt it."

"I could have." He shrugged stiffly. "You weren't exactly guarding your coffee last night."

"I want to believe it's more than that."

"Why, Mulder?"

Grey laughed. "I walked into that one." There was a fevered glitter to his eyes, a breathless rush to his words. "If it's true, then I really can help you. I really can do something good with this. It will have meaning."

Meaning? *Meaning*? He couldn't mean anything if he was dead! Saint bit his lip, shaking his head. "You're that eager to be a ritual sacrifice?"

"No." Again that laugh, sweet and joyous; hardly the laugh of a dead man walking. "No, it's not about that at all."

"You still won't tell me what it's about."

"You've got your secrets. I've got mine." Grey drew him close, kissed him: fierce and hard and sweet-hot as a burning cherry, searing his mouth and leaving behind the inescapable wildness of his taste. "Saint. *Saint.*"

He backed Saint against the wall, pinning him roughly against weathered wood, rough edges snagging on his shirt and biting into his back. He stared up at Grey, outlined dark against the halo of the sun, unable to help arching as Grey's body crushed into his, sliding hard and slow, stroking every inch of him in a full-body caress that left him painfully aware of Grey's heat, the thick pressure thrusting against his jeans, his deepwater scent. He smelled like the dreams of a leviathan, gliding dark and slow, stealing into Saint until his pulse raced and his vision swam with a sudden dizzy rush of that warmth that had shocked him into such sharp awareness. Heated lips grazed his neck, and he sucked in a raw breath that cut the inside of his throat.

"Grey...?"

"Here," Grey whispered, clutching Saint's hips, and jerked him closer. His hands slid down Saint's thighs, cupped underneath, lifted him off his feet and wrapped his legs around Grey's waist until there was nothing holding him up but the sharp perfect pleasure of Grey's body clasped between his thighs and the feeling of intimacy when he was spread open and held so close. "Right here. I need you."

He should say no. He *had* to say no, but the words were lost inside him, swallowed in this need that infected him. Too quick, too soon, from one sweet kiss to this savage desire, but he couldn't stop it. If the passion had ahold of Grey, it had Saint too—and without another word, he cradled Grey's jaw, dragged that sinful mouth up from his throat, and kissed him.

If their first kiss was sugar, then this one was hot molasses rum, an intoxicating burn that poured down his throat and spread fire in his belly. Grey kissed him like a man possessed, his lust a drugging cloud enveloping Saint. He breathed it in like pheromones and ambrosia and let it get deep under his skin, until he was panting and fucking high on the crushing lock of their lips and the way Grey's tongue slipped into him and lit sparks on every stroking, invading caress.

"Grey," he gasped, locking his arms tight around him, digging his fingers into Grey's back, stroking his thighs against Grey's waist and twisting his hips until the next time their bodies crashed together it hit *just* right and friction dragged along his cock, the soft cotton weave of his boxers wrapping around him in a sheath and making him cry out with pleasure as the pressure of Grey's body trapped him. "Grey!"

Grey's only answer was a low groan—and the rake of rough, desperate hands over Saint's body, fingers digging into his thighs, his hips, his waist, his chest, leaving trails of electric heat. Saint sucked in a breath as one dark hand worked past the waist of his jeans and pulled *hard*, denim biting painfully into his skin only to go slack, the pain easing, as with a *snap* the button flew off and the zipper tore free and suddenly he was fighting with Grey to drag his pants down his thighs and off without ever letting go.

Saint's boxers tore. One shoe tumbled off. Clothing dropped in shreds to the ground. He didn't care, as hot summer air licked its damp mouth over naked skin and he whimpered with every touch of Grey's exploring fingers over his cock. Those long artist's hands enveloped him so fully; he tossed his head back against the weathered pinewood, choked on the scent of sex riding the musty afternoon, and lifted his hips into every touch that commanded his senses and drew up tight in that low place where his pleasure centered, just below his cock and pulsing deeper than flesh.

"Bondye," Grey breathed. "You're so fucking beautiful like this. Mesmerizing. Is this how you inspire people?"

Saint opened his eyes to find Grey watching him with an intensity that bordered on fixation, his expression as rapt as if he'd seen the face of his loa. No one had ever looked at Saint that way. Not even Arturo, devout Arturo who wore his priest's vestments to write, and thought his words were a gift from God. Saint couldn't stand it. Couldn't stand being looked at that way and wondering if this madness was real, when all he wanted was the heated pleasure of Grey's fingers on his skin and the pressure building inside him to a break point.

"Don't. Don't ask me that right now." He closed his eyes again, biting back a moan, lifting himself into Grey's touch. "Don't make it about that."

Grey's hold stilled, gripping firmly. His thumb circled the head of Saint's cock, teasing delicately at the sensitive places just underneath, and he writhed, panting, as torment rolled through him in shivering waves and painful little stabs of pleasure each time Grey flicked in just . . . the right . . . *spot*.

"Do you want me, Saint?"

"Yes. *Yes.*"

Grey released him. He opened his eyes to protest—only to find Grey fishing a small clear bottle of translucent fluid from his back pocket. "Let me touch you."

"Why do you keep lube in your—"

A fierce grin parted Grey's lips. "Is that really the question you want to be asking at the moment?"

Mute, Saint shook his head—only to tense as Grey cupped his ass in broad hands, kneaded, gripped. He tried to brace himself, but there was no anticipating the pad of a coarse fingertip brushing his entrance, teasingly light, only to dart away . . . and return slicked in lubricant, probing and massaging in sharp shocks of sensitivity so keen they were almost uncomfortable, embarrassing, and he flushed and turned his face away, biting his lip *hard* on a cry as that wet-oiled, warm finger sank inside.

He couldn't stand it. The sweet stretching sensation, the slow plunge deeper, *deeper*, slipping into him as if Grey had every right to be there and stroking him from within. He dug his fingers into Grey's shoulders and lifted his hips with a cry. Another finger. Another, long and agile and curling inside him, exploring, touching him in places that made the insides of his eyelids burst with color and his mouth ache with the pain of his biting teeth, trying so hard not to scream and yet failing. He could taste his own cracking whimper, and it tasted like the pleasure and agony of those deft fingers filling him, working his body, twisting and thrusting and taunting him with that slick hot sinful rhythm.

Grey's mouth skimmed his throat, his jaw, adding sparks to flame with each brushing touch, with the rough, desire-darkened heat of his voice in Saint's ear. "How much more can you endure?"

He tossed his head and clenched his thighs against Grey's hips. "No more—no more!"

"I could stop." Those maddening fingers slowed, stopped, buried so deep. "If it's so terrible."

"Don't you *dare.*"

"Say it," Grey demanded.

Saint opened his eyes, looking up into burnished gold that glowed with a fervor that bordered on fury. This was the darkness he'd seen in Grey's paintings. The blackness that was light without light, a soul buried in an endless night and finding beauty in the gloom. This fire was what had made him choose Grey—a fire he only wished was fueled by a will to live.

A fire he wanted to have for his own, if only for a little while.

"Take me," he said, and drew Grey down to kiss him.

He felt the throbbing absence of touch as Grey's fingers slipped from his body. Then the rasp of a zipper, the slick press of hot flesh sliding together, the thick head of Grey's cock nudging against his belly and pushing his shirt up and leaving a warm, wet trail on his skin. He lifted himself, surrendered himself into Grey's grip as the other man positioned him just right—wanting it, needing it, close to begging for it when Grey gave him everything he craved. Pain split him open, forcing heavy and deep, rushing the breath from his lungs and leaving him drowning in the tight, aching feeling of being too *full.* Too full with Grey; too full with these rough, tumbling emotions that tore at him with howling claws.

The lock of their bodies came together so perfectly, and filled him with a pleasure like madness. It took his senses, reshaped them, reshaped *him* until he existed only for the searing thrust of Grey's cock inside him, until his heart beat to the rhythm of crash and roll and flow until he didn't know if he was moving Grey or Grey was moving him or they were moving together. Every thrust shocked through him with quick-flash jolts that left him brimming, trembling, alive with something . . . something greater than himself. Something arcane, something primal, something as ancient as the song of the stars and the burn of the sun that beat down on their flesh and witnessed this thing that rolled between them like ritual and worship, travesty and blessed benediction.

He was burnt offerings smoldering at Grey's altar, locked to him inescapably. Bound one to another, until Grey's pleasure was his pleasure, until Grey's breaths were his breaths, until Grey's cries were his cries. In this moment, Grey was with him down to their very bones, a geas wrought in pleasure and bittersweet emotion that swept him high and brought him low. He tried to resist. Tried to hold back.

But when Grey pinned him harder to the wall, when he felt the swelling that promised a flood of liquid-burning slickness, when Grey's fingers wrapped around his cock and demanded . . .

He shattered to pieces, and knew he would never be able to resist Grey anything.

For the rest of his short, numbered days.

✳ 24 ✳

Grey thought he was going to pass out.

He also thought he might be able to smell colors and taste sounds. He wasn't even sure which way was up, right now. He sagged against Saint, his entire body throbbing in the aftermath and his senses scrambled. They'd *been* scrambled since he picked up that brush, and only now after he'd spent himself was everything starting to make sense again. If he'd been high as fuck before, this was what coming down must feel like, and he hurt deep in his bones as he gathered Saint close and tried to catch his heaving breaths.

He felt like something had shifted at his core, moving aside to make room for Saint, and he would never be the same again.

"Grey." Saint gripped at his arms, and Grey realized he was still *inside* him, almost too numb and drained to feel it, and swore out an apology.

"Fuck. Sorry. Sorry."

He pulled back, gently lowering Saint's legs to the ground, contrition on his lips for Saint's pained hiss—only to burst into panicked curses again as he saw the slick of glistening fluid on pale inner thighs.

"Fuck, we didn't use a—"

"It's fine." A shallow imitation of a smile flickered across Saint's lips. He bent, wincing, and retrieved his jeans and torn boxers. "I can't get sick. Nothing you have can infect me. I don't have anything to infect you. Otherwise I'd have every back-alley brothel disease from the eighteenth century."

Grey tried a laugh, but it scratched his throat. These mundane words, after he'd broken every piece of himself with the force of his need for Saint . . . it didn't feel right. "I . . ."

The words he'd wanted fell away. There was nothing in their space, blank and clouded; he couldn't even remember what he'd wanted to talk about. He closed his eyes, but that didn't stop the vertigo from taking a spin round his skull.

"I can't . . . remember what I meant to say. My head feels— Whoa." He reeled, and shot a hand out to brace against the wall.

"Yes. That happens." A soft touch feathered against his arm. He opened his eyes to find Saint dressed and watching him with concern, something shielded in those liquid eyes. "Inside. I'll make you something to drink. It will help . . . temporarily."

"Temporarily?"

"Tea cannot restore the lost years of your life," Saint murmured and, with a lingering look, turned and slipped inside the house.

Grey followed him. The edges of the world had a certain glassiness to them, but that didn't stop him from seeing the dark, rotting emptiness of the house's interior. Cobwebs festooned the house, covering peeling walls and cracking rafters and the mildewed, tattered remnants of furniture, each room dusty as a mummy's rags. The fusty smell nearly choked him; the floorboards creaked under every step. He pulled his shirt up over his mouth, fighting to hold his tongue. How could Saint *live* here?

The steps they mounted were cleaner—more recently repaired, many replaced with fresh white pine planks. They curved upstairs in a spiral; Saint led him past the second floor, moving with a faint limp that might have left Grey smug with satisfaction if he weren't struggling to stay conscious. Higher, past the third floor, until the stairs narrowed on a small passageway that opened into, he thought, one of the towers he'd seen from outside.

Saint pushed the door open on a self-contained wonderland.

If the house was falling apart, the circular tower room was carefully preserved—along with everything in it. Books and knickknacks that had to be centuries old, a hoarder's trove of odds and ends ranging from hand-painted globes to an old typewriter to an entire row of nineteenth-century dolls set along the fireplace mantel. *Things* occupied every surface, each like a bookmark in the pages of a life longer than Grey could comprehend. Tapestries draped the walls in patterns from the Middle East, interspersed with bits of clothing that had gone out of style a century ago—waistcoats and fitted jackets and breeches waiting to be worn again—all wound about with ivy vines that Grey thought might be plastic but could just as easily be real. The faint, musky scent of some kind of oil filled the air.

The room lit up with stars when Saint flicked a switch and the Christmas lights strung in tangles across the ceiling came to life—as well as lamps with holes carefully poked in the shades, filtering tiny, glowing dots. The entire space was colored in wine and gold and shadow, and those lights only brought out the subtle, shimmering inflections of each hue.

Grey turned slowly, taking everything in, and reached out to gently trace the glass curve of a ship in a bottle, set atop an ancient, curling parchment map spread over a desk as if that ship were sailing the blue-inked seas.

"This is your life," he murmured, then jumped as, with a tinny whistle, an electric toy train zipped past his shoulder, the track mounted on the wall. "It's . . . like a catalog of lifetimes."

"Something like that. Here." Saint's hand pressed to his back and guided him to a long, low chaise. "Sit."

Grey sank down against the plush burgundy cushions and watched helplessly as Saint crossed the layered Persian rugs to a little bolt-on modern kitchenette built into the wall. His movements were jerky as he filled a kettle, his shoulders taut, his eyes downcast. Grey's throat knotted. This . . . wasn't how it was supposed to be, after the first time. He'd wanted to just hold Saint and breathe in the sweat on his skin and feel his body cooling as he came down, and instead here they were, standing in tense opposition in the silence.

"You're upset," he said.

"I'm not."

"You are." No answer. "I've hurt you." A flinch, but Saint's back remained to him. "Saint. Tell me what I did."

Saint's spine stiffened, but he said nothing as he set out mugs and began doling tea bags and sugar into them. Until he set a spoon down inside a mug with a *clank*, and tilted his head back with a grudging sigh.

"It took you," he said. The flat, matter-of-fact tone was all wrong. "And then you took *me*. You came here *prepared* for that. Pragmatic, the lubricant. I suppose I should admire your sensibility, considering you were hardly in control of your faculties."

"Oh." Realization rolled its ten-ton weight through Grey's gut. "You thought . . . the only reason I . . . Oh." His mouth dried. He sat back hard against the arm of the chaise. "Then why didn't you say no?"

Saint shrugged bitterly. "Have to eat, don't I?"

"*No.*" Horror choked his throat. While he'd been so caught in something that felt like it shook his world with how beautiful it was, how beautiful Saint was . . . Saint had just been enduring it to live? "Bondye, no. I won't be a rapist. I can't. If I'd known you— If I—"

"Grey." Saint left the tea and crossed the room to sink to his knees before him. Slim hands enveloped his own, and he hadn't realized he was cold until their heat nearly burned him. Saint looked up at him earnestly. "I was willing. You didn't rape me."

He shook his head. "I don't understand."

"You only wanted me because your inspiration had you." Sunset eyes lowered to their clasped hands. "Maybe I wanted you for other reasons."

Several seconds ticked by before Grey realized what Saint was saying. Painful seconds, seconds of doubt, seconds of despair, until it sank in:

Saint was saying he wanted him. Not just his life, not just this bargain.

Him.

Relief and warmth fought for dominance inside him, and he spilled off the couch to his knees, thudding down against the layered carpets. "No. No, Saint." He gathered him close, pulling his stiff, resisting form into his arms, begging him with touch to relax, to let go of that quiet pride and just let Grey hold him. "I've wanted you since I opened my eyes and all I could see was you, filmed through blood. I lay there dying, and all I could think of was the feeling of your hands on my chest. White birds, fluttering against me." His heart faltered, echoed muscle memory of those struggling moments when it had almost stopped. He buried his face against Saint's throat. "I've always been this way. After a day of painting, when inspiration strikes . . . I want to share the intensity I'm feeling with someone close to me. Painting is an intimate thing, for me. It . . . amplifies what I'm already feeling. That's all it was. I *wanted* you. No motivation other than that."

Slowly, that slender body went soft against him. Slowly, slim arms crept around him. Slowly, Saint's head sank to rest against his shoulder, breaths washing warm against his throat.

"Am I . . . You . . . think of me as close to you?" Saint whispered, and that broken, childlike hesitancy in his voice nearly crushed Grey's heart.

"There are few things more intimate than sharing a death." He closed his eyes and held Saint tighter; some deep, secret part of him wished he never had to let go. "There is no one who could ever be closer to me than you, Saint. No one at all."

✳⊱ 25 ⊰✳

They curled together on the chaise, and Saint hated himself more with every moment he watched Grey's fingers tremble on the mug until Saint reached up to hold it steady, lifting it to his lips.

"Thank you." Grey's laugh was shaky. "I feel like an old man."

"It doesn't normally happen this fast. One kiss and it took you; one time together, and you're already weak."

"Perhaps it's because I know." Grey leaned over and rested his temple to Saint's. "Perhaps it's because I accept it. I accept you. I chose you."

Saint clutched his own mug close, as if its heat could warm the layer of ice trying to squeeze his heart. "How can you be so calm about it? I've spent two centuries terrified of dying. And you just . . . *accept* it."

"It's easy to accept something that's seemed inevitable for so long." Grey shrugged. "I don't know. It feels . . . logical, somehow."

"That's it. You wake up one day and decide it would be logical for you to die."

"Something like that." A strained smile. "It's complicated."

"As complicated as a man with no memory stealing others' lives to survive?"

"I'd say they're on an equal level." Soft breaths stirred Saint's hair as Grey nuzzled into him. "I think we complicate each other quite nicely."

"Most people aren't fond of complications."

"I like them. Complications are . . . colorful." Grey took a sip of his tea. "The world I'd meant to leave behind was empty of color. Gray and empty. I'd rather the last thing I know be a world of colors, full and beautiful."

"Won't that make you regret leaving it more?"

"How long can you regret something when you're dead?"

Not nearly as long as you can when you can never die.

Saint shook his head with a noncommittal sound and tucked his legs up against his side, burrowing into Grey. After a few moments, one warm, heavy arm fell over his shoulders, and he closed his eyes and breathed in the steam from his tea and told himself he couldn't feel Grey's trembling.

"My granmé used to say regret is a mistake the living make," Grey murmured. "You've only got so long, so don't waste that time regretting what you didn't do. If you *do* it . . . what you did will still be there when you're gone. Do nothing . . . and nothing is left behind."

"You speak of her often. She must be important to you."

"She was."

Something in Grey's voice made Saint look up. "'Was'...?"

"You aren't the only one who doesn't have anyone left." Grey's gaze unfocused, seeing far things. Old things, Saint thought, but not forgotten, and for a moment he was jealous that Grey *knew* his past, his people. "My grandmother and grandfather immigrated here from Haiti in the forties. But they went back to the homeland to retire. Years later, so did my parents. That was before the earthquake." His jaw tightened on a swallow. "I'm an only child. And all of my extended family..."

"I'm sorry," Saint murmured, though it felt like cold comfort.

"I hadn't seen them in years. I was selfish. Too focused on my art to see that they wouldn't always be there. I kept promising I'd visit next year, and then next year, and then..." Grey trailed off, but the hitch in his breath gave him away.

"Everyone's allowed to be selfish." He rested a hand to Grey's chest. "We can't know what will happen. And we can't blame ourselves for things beyond our control."

"Not seeing them ... that was in my control. I chose to make something else more important."

"And now you choose how you die, before that choice can be taken away." Tentatively, he reached up to press his palm to the sharp, warm angles of Grey's cheek, and was rewarded by Grey leaning into him, rubbing a scratchy cheek against his hand. "You still have the memories. That's something."

Grey's eyes closed. "I think I would give anything not to remember."

"You only say that because you don't know what it's like." So bitter, to want what Grey would willingly give up. The back of his throat tasted foul. "You don't know what it's like to have a hole inside you where everything you've ever loved should be."

"Maybe not," Grey whispered, and pressed his lips to Saint's palm. "But I know what it's like to feel empty. To feel as if I've lost everything. So I paint for the loa, because I have no one else. To be loved by the loa is to love and be loved by the dead. I love my dead, and so I paint the loa."

"Does it fill that emptiness?"

"Sometimes. Sometimes, nothing does." Grey's eyes opened, nearly glowing in the deep shadows of the tower room: mesmerizing, compelling, and Saint pleaded silently for that light to never go out. "Is it strange that I feel the least empty when I'm with you?"

"A little." Saint smiled faintly. "All things considered . . . is it strange that that makes me happy?"

"No." Grey's mouth moved against his palm, praying the words into his skin. "If I leave nothing else behind but that, then I've done enough."

€ 26 ꝫ

The weakness hadn't lasted as long as Grey expected. He'd drifted off with Saint on the couch, and woken up feeling as if he'd survived a plague that swept through the night and was gone by morning: his body strange, but his own again—for now.

He'd thought to kiss Saint goodbye, and return to his studio. Thought to take this slow, day by day. But instead, with the taste of Saint still lingering on his lips and something inside him threatening to break at the thought of separation, he said, "Come with me."

Be with me.

He'd said it on impulse, but the moment he did, the moment those haunted eyes widened and stared at him with such vulnerability, he knew it was right. If his time was limited, he wanted to spend each moment he could like this:

With sunset eyes looking up at him, seeing him . . . and, for the first time in far too long, easing the numbness and reminding him how to feel.

€ 27 ꝫ

The first day in Grey's apartment, Saint didn't know what to do with himself.

He was accustomed to becoming the wallpaper of his victims' lives, convincing himself he was their lover and their beloved and not just an afterthought to what truly mattered most. He wondered now if he'd been punishing himself, even if he'd refused to acknowledge it. Enduring the bitterness and the isolation and the ache as part of his penance for what he was, for what came next. Sooner or later he always found a routine, settling in to this farce of domesticity in which he worked and lived the solitary life of the forgotten, alone even when they were together—and coming home each day to find them spent and tired and yet still struggling to eke out just one last drop of blood and turn it into magic.

But *sooner or later* wasn't *now*, and right now he was standing in a home that wasn't his own while Grey looked at him as if he could see nothing else. Saint fidgeted uncomfortably as he stepped off the elevator and into the apartment. Grey wasn't supposed to *see* him, right now. He was supposed to be fixated on his paints, his visions. And as lonely as it had been to be forgotten by everyone before . . . it was fucking uncomfortable to be the center of someone's attention after two centuries of being a shadow.

He couldn't stand it anymore. He knotted his fingers in the strap of his overnight bag and glared at Grey. "*What?*"

Grey had been parting his lips to speak, but froze, blinking. ". . . What?"

"You're looking at me again!"

"You don't want me to?"

He scowled. "I'm afraid you'll start spouting poetry or something."

With a smirk, Grey folded his arms over his chest. "I'm mildly fascinated. I haven't lost my fucking mind."

"*Mildly?*" Saint's eyes narrowed. His mouth twitched in that tight way it did when he was trying not to smile, fighting his lips, but they kept pulling upward. "I'm insulted."

Grey only looked at him flatly, skeptically, before that smirk widened into a grin—an infectious one, a contagious one, full of the warmth Saint had been starved of for so long, and before he could stop himself, he laughed, looking away and covering his face with one hand as if he could somehow hide it. As if he weren't allowed, in this situation, to feel anything this light, this normal, this sweetly embarrassed.

"That's better." Grey chuckled and slid an arm around his shoulder. "Relax. I don't mean to make you uncomfortable. I'm just . . . thinking. Turning this over. Absorbing the situation, and you. I suppose putting a countdown on everything makes me more focused."

Mumbling, Saint leaned tentatively into the crook of Grey's arm. "You're not supposed to be focused on *me*."

"Why not?"

"I just . . . I'm not . . ."

"Not what?"

"I'm not something that fascinates people." He caught his tongue between his teeth, lowering his eyes. "I'm not the thing that people love. Not really. I'm just a means to an end. That's how this works."

"I'm changing how it works. And if you call yourself a *thing* one more time," Grey said fiercely, "I'm taking you over my knee."

He laughed weakly. "Promise?"

"That would be an appealing prospect if you weren't deflecting."

"You're the second person to call me on that in as many days."

Grey caught his chin lightly in rough-tipped fingers, tilting his face up to meet Grey's eyes, looking into him in that way that made Saint feel too exposed. "So stop doing it."

"Why?"

"What are you afraid to show me, when I'll take your secrets to the grave?"

Saint didn't know why his eyes brimmed at that. Why they burned. Why *he* burned, crumbling to ash inside when all Grey was offering was wordless, simple understanding. He only knew he couldn't let himself break down again, because he was already bracing for the pain of loss, already shuttering himself in to weather the storm of grief that would come when the quiet light left those searching, earnest eyes.

So he pulled away, turned his back on Grey, and reached up to smooth his fingers through his hair just to give his hands something to do other than clutch on to Grey and beg him not to die.

"Show me what you painted," he said thickly.

In the pregnant silence, he could sense the things unsaid. The questions unasked. The need unanswered. But Grey only strode past him without a word, leading him to the studio area and brushing aside the curtain. A new canvas leaned against the wall, a tall square in shimmering darkness. Grey shifted uneasily and looked away from it.

"Here."

Saint stepped closer. A chill shot through him, his skin crackling like hoarfrost, and he hugged his arms tighter to himself as if he could ward it off when it was coming from inside.

Deep-set eyes stared into him from the canvas, burning with an unspoken vow. With an unvoiced *need*, a consuming hunger for a darkness that could so easily swallow them both. His stomach twisted, and he closed his eyes against that wide jackal's grin, that painted skull-face, that sense of aching familiarity at once beautiful and horrific. That there was passion in this painting, there was no doubt. That it was *Grey's* passion . . .

What was he pulling out of this man, just by being in his life?

"Who is that?" he whispered.

"Bawon Samedi." Grey spoke the name with that same soft reverence as when he'd spoken of Erzulie, and of giving his love to his loa. "You'd probably compare him to the Grim Reaper. He is death, and beloved for it."

"He frightens me."

"Why?"

Saint opened his eyes, and met that haunted, needful gaze again. First on the canvas . . . and then in the very real, living eyes that fixed on him, capturing him in Grey.

"Because he looks like you," he said.

✳ 28 ✳

For a while, Grey remembered what it was like to be bright.

Even as he painted out the dark inside him, he remembered what it was like to be bright. What it was like to laugh over Chinese takeout, and watch Saint's face light up when Grey poked him in the nose with his chopsticks. What it was like to live somewhere that wasn't empty, when Saint gently occupied every nook and cranny with a living warmth, the scents of flesh, the sounds of *being*.

What it was like to kiss someone, and lose himself in the consuming feeling, breathing it inside him like incense smoke and the breath of the loa.

Saint wasn't a cure for what had broken inside him. Wasn't a cure for anything but that persistent disease of life. But he was a New Thing, a beautiful thing, and Grey had learned that sometimes a New Thing could disrupt that channel in his brain enough to shake his thoughts loose and let them flood free, giving him a few moments of respite before everything ran back downhill and found its flat, empty equilibrium again.

Happiness, he'd found, was a temporary state. Something he had to steal, something he had to savor while he had it, because he didn't know when it would slip through his fingers and not return for days or weeks or years.

Years.

He thought of Aminata as he traced the outline of a swelling breast and the slope of a gently curving arm in soft, light sketch lines. He thought of Aminata, counted the years, wondered where she was, and buried himself in Saint to try to forget.

He painted: every waking moment, every sleeping one, pushing himself until he could no longer stand. Sometimes those fevered spells lasted days. Sometimes only hours before he was swaying against the wall, gasping, watching as the tendons in his arms turned into rails and imagining he could see them shrivel and wither with each minute instead of each day. More than once, Saint had to help him to bed, dab his brow. Part of him didn't believe it was real.

But part of him knew he was wasting away inside, until he was just a shell of a man glowing with the fire that lit him from within—even as that fire burned him out to nothing.

Still, he painted. He painted, then took Saint into his arms and loved him with a ferocity that bordered on desperation, because it wasn't his art driving his passion. It was knowing that when the colors were in his blood, when the music of brushstrokes guided the beat of his heart, that lovely man was waiting for him, watching him from a perch against the windowsill, *knowing* him with every piece of his soul he cut out of himself to leave on the canvas as yet another aspect of Bawon Samedi's ghastly beautiful face. He didn't need those pieces anymore.

That was what was wrong with people, he thought. They guarded their souls so jealously, as if they were afraid if they gave too much they'd just be empty vessels by the time Samedi came for them.

Grey would empty himself out, then. Willingly. Empty himself in colors, empty himself in Saint, and he whispered his name over and over again as he stroked paint-streaked fingers through his hair and kissed his cheeks, his jaw, his mouth.

"I can't think of anything but you," he whispered. "Even when I paint . . . it's only you. How are you doing this to me?"

Saint shook his head, his eyes gleaming unnaturally bright in the darkness of Grey's apartment, the shadows cast over the bed. "I don't know." His voice broke. "That's not how it's supposed to be. I thought I'd have more time to know you. Not . . . this. Not watching you disappear through my fingers. You're water, and I can't hold on to you no matter how hard I try."

"How is it supposed to be? Am I not supposed to feed you?"

"You're only supposed to use me," Saint said. "Until I use you to death."

✳ɞ 29 ʒ✳

They leaned back to back in the window seat in Grey's apartment, wrapped in the same blanket and naked in their own cooling sweat. Saint tilted his head against Grey's shoulder and looked up at the rows of hanging lights in their mason jars, the clouded glass turning the light dusty as sun shafts on a dry Savannah afternoon. He still ached, sore inside from what Grey had done to him, yet the pain was secondary to the feeling of life burning through his veins, too hot, filling up the empty spaces inside. He could feel the vibrato tenor of the other man's longing rising off him in silent notes, his restless need to get up, to paint, to give an outlet to the fire Saint had kindled inside him.

Yet here Grey was, staying. His shoulder blades spread like the hard-edged wings of a seagull against Saint's back, more stark than they'd been a week ago; sweat mixed in the channels of their spines.

He hated feeling the parchment fragility of Grey's skin stretched over such prominent bones, but he couldn't pull away. Not even in those moments when Grey arched over him, and the sunken hollows beneath his eyes belonged to the skull-faced man he painted over and over again with every new piece.

What was Grey trying to say to him by staying? By not leaving him alone, to spend his last hours living for his art?

Was he trying to prove that he *saw* Saint, when no one else truly had?

The days were passing too fast. He didn't know how it was happening—how between his shifts and those quiet nights, somehow the days had melted away and taken Grey's life with them. Later, when he looked back on this, he would remember late-night conversations. Lying in bed with their fingers twined, while he told Grey of every man he'd loved. Whispered to him of how the light would catch Arturo's jaw, or how Philippe had always managed to lose *just one* shoe and never find it again. He told him the stories of his past: of what had once been, the ghosts that occupied the same space as the familiar Savannah that Grey knew. He told him of his now, too: of the half-drowned girl who'd cried and hugged him after he and Nuo had resuscitated her, of how he'd hidden himself in the locker room and sobbed when they hadn't been able to do enough to save a single one of the victims in a drunk-driving accident, of how in that moment he'd wished for Grey's hand, just to make it hurt a little less.

He'd never let anyone know him like this before. Not all of him. Everyone he'd ever known only saw the colors of a single patchwork square, and not the pattern they made when stitched together.

But Grey saw his colors, saw his patterns, and still dug deeper. Still begged for more, as if he could take Saint into himself to replace what he lost hour by hour, minute by minute.

Why are you doing this? Saint had asked, as their legs had tangled and he laid his head to Grey's shoulder.

Doing what?

Trying to be with me.

Grey had traced the line of his cheekbone, and threaded his fingers into his hair. *I* am *with you, Saint. I'm asking you to be with me.*

I am with you.

Are you?

If I wasn't, you wouldn't be dying.

He let the blanket slip aside enough to look down at his own shoulder. The lines blooming there were faint, but growing darker by the day. A stag, proud and elegant, with moon-silver fur and coyote eyes. This would be his memory of Grey, then, and he traced the forming lines with his fingertips and wondered that they felt like the coarseness of Grey's stubble under his touch.

"This isn't supposed to feel real," Saint whispered.

"I know." Grey tilted his head back as well, until they rested cheek to cheek. "But it does."

✳ 30 ✳

So this is what it feels like to die.

Grey was alone, tonight. Saint had been called out on an early extra shift, barely a moment to pause and kiss Grey's brow before he rattled down the elevator to sling himself into the passenger's seat of Nuo's car—a pale figure against the night, watched from the upstairs window. The warmth of his lips still burned Grey's skin; the only warmth he'd been able to grasp lately, when he felt so very, very cold. He touched his fingers to his forehead, traced the shape of Saint's mouth in body heat. Strange, how over barely two weeks such little gestures had become familiar. Normal.

All of this was somehow too normal. The daily routine of dying. Like any other job it took work, time, and patience.

With a laugh under his breath, he tucked himself against the couch and wrapped himself in blankets that did little to stave off the chill that had, just like the weakness and the shakes, become his new normal. Across the apartment, several blank canvases waited in his studio, but they held no appeal for him tonight. His hands ached, his heart sore and tired, and he felt Saint's absence like a hole in space-time.

Not long now, he thought, and spread his fingers. The webbing between had grown translucent, a fine skim of skin with barely any color at all. Maybe he really was crazy, that he felt such relief. Such contentment, to know that he was almost there. Yet there was a quiet melancholy too, at the idea of leaving Saint behind. Of not being here for him, to hold his hand through the grief and kiss his tears away, when Grey himself was the cause of those tears.

And fear, muted and low, a whisper he tried to ignore. The beginning of a question, a *What if* without the other half, hanging open-ended and waiting for him to give it space to become something real.

He couldn't. He wouldn't. He'd made his choice, and there was no turning back now.

He fished his phone from his pocket with clumsy fingers and scrolled through his contacts, then paused before he'd even passed one screen. There it was, right under the *As. Aminata.* Once, years ago, they'd sat on the edge of the fountain together and watched midnight tick over with the sky lit up in gold and red and violet as one second made the difference between one year and the next, with their bare feet dabbling in the cool water and Grey's toes going numb from the wet winter chill.

She'd looked at him sideways and smiled her little smile that always meant she was thinking. *Hey, Grey?*

Yeah, Ami?

How come we don't never fall in love?

He'd laughed and leaned over to press his shoulder to hers. Back then laughing had been easier, and hadn't felt like something he just had to fake to get by; he'd felt it behind his eyes, when he chuckled and wrapped his arm around her shoulder to tuck her against his side. *We got love. You don't want to fuck that up by going at it the wrong way, do you?*

She'd watched him, her eyes strange. *No. No, guess I don't.*

He'd kissed the top of her head and held her tight and hoped, in that moment, nothing would change even though by then *he* was already changing. And deep down he'd known it was the start of something, something big, but he'd never thought their continental drift would take them to entirely separate worlds. He'd never thought he would let it happen so easily, but that dulling filter had fallen down and he'd turned listless and slow, and some days it took more than he had the capacity for to pick up the phone. Then *some days* became *every day*, and *every day* became *one day*, and one day . . .

One day, she was just gone.

He supposed Saint wasn't the only one haunted by memories of people who'd passed from his life.

What would she say, if he reached out and made that connection again? If he tried to remember what it was like to have a friend?

Would she even want to hear it if he said goodbye?

That question hovered too close to the edge of that *What if*, threatened to fall over. He shook it off and scrolled to Saint's contact and tapped a text, each word picked out slowly when the screen would hardly register contact with his weak, flickering body heat.

Am I supposed to miss you like this?

Nearly ten minutes passed before his phone buzzed in response. Just a single word, fading onto the screen. *Don't.*

Don't what? he tapped back.

Don't miss me.

Why not?

No answer. Not for over an hour, not until he'd almost fallen asleep, his head rolling back on a neck that didn't really want to support it. His eyes lidded heavy, gritty and tired, before snapping open as his phone vibrated again. Letters scrolled up the screen, and in them he could hear Saint's lilting voice, dark with a pain and recrimination that made him wonder if he was doing the right thing, made that *What if* into a painful question of *What if I decide to live?*

Because, Saint wrote, *it will make it that much harder to miss you.*

✳ 31 ✳

It wasn't supposed to happen so quickly.

Saint watched Grey sleep. His breaths rattled. His chest sank in just a little too much when he exhaled, and the graceful hollows under his cheekbones had become pits. Still he was beautiful, but he was shriveling like a rose deprived of the sun—and it had only been *three weeks*.

"Not yet," he whispered, and traced the line of Grey's jaw. "Please don't leave me yet."

Grey only breathed deeper, a wheezing, horrible thing, and Saint pulled away. He couldn't stand the evidence of this. Of what he was doing to Grey, even as Saint grew stronger by the day.

He slid out of the bed, the muggy night air licking over his naked skin, swirling sluggishly in from the open windows. Grey's studio area waited like a gallery of ghosts, silver moonlight washing the dark shadows of his paintings with an ashen glow. Saint leaned against the windowsill and looked into the eyes of a woman painted in lush curves, her arms lined with the sprouting features of a black rooster, her hair a spreading galaxy of stars, her breasts supported by the curving arcs of stark ribs, bone gleaming white on black skin. Grey had called her Maman Brigitte, and said she was the wife of the man he painted like a haunting spirit, waiting around every corner.

Bawon Samedi.

Always, always Grey painted death.

Saint lost himself in looking into her deep black eyes. Why just the one of her? Why was she different? What was in this painting that made it seem, for just a moment, Grey had wanted something different when he turned not to the father, but the mother of the dead?

He hardly heard Grey rising, but he felt his warmth as the other man slipped his arms around Saint's waist and rested his chin to his shoulder.

"You're up," Grey murmured.

"Couldn't sleep."

"So you look at my nightmares instead?"

"To me, they only look like dreams."

He met Grey's eyes sidelong, but Grey looked away. A broad, dark hand spread over Saint's stomach, and he sucked in a breath as it stroked, hot as livid coals, up over his chest. Splayed fingertips traced the patterns of his tattoos, delicately following each line over his shoulders, down his arms.

"Tell me what these mean," Grey whispered against his skin, and Saint leaned back into him.

"They're my memories." He stretched one arm out, turning it so that the creatures painted across his skin twisted and writhed as if alive. "They're the part of you that I take into myself." He followed the swirling feathers of the firebird, mapping it by touch, coiling from his wrist to his elbow. "This was Jake." Higher. Over the Quetzalcoatl on his biceps, to that stag slowly fading into existence on his shoulder. "And this is you."

Grey studied the tattoo, then smiled and kissed just below it. "I like it." Soft lips, softer words traced Saint's skin, and he melted as nips left stinging warmth along the line of his collarbone, marking each sighing sound. "All in black and white. So stark and unforgiving, your world."

Slowly, Grey pulled away, leaving Saint cold, reaching for him—until Grey picked up a palette, a brush, his smile warming as he crooked a finger.

"Let me paint your colors."

Saint drifted closer. Uncertain, he flicked his gaze from the brush to the palette as Grey dipped the bristles into a gleaming pool of burnt umber, then swirled it into a wash of red until the colors spiraled around each other. Something in the way Grey looked at him transfixed him, and he held himself so very still as the other man reached out with the brush and touched it to his skin. The slick paint streaked over his flesh with a cold, feathering shock, and he gasped, tensing.

"Shh," Grey breathed. His eyes lidded, his focus a palpable thing, a third presence in the room, wrapping Saint in the intensity of it. Grey could be *consuming* when he turned the entirety of his attention on Saint—an overwhelming thing that made him feel like the object of a beautiful fixation, a sick obsession, a wondrous addiction, a binding that linked them so inextricably. And with that focus on him now, he could hardly breathe as the tip of the brush tickled and licked over his skin, so delicately following the lines of the firebird, filling in the white spaces between with swirling streaks of red and gold.

Saint trembled. Jake's tattoo. A brand marking his past, just like all the others. Each life, each death, each memory held close. Yet now Grey transformed it into something new, the phoenix coming alive in fiery shades, vibrant and shimmering with the glistening sheen Grey stroked onto his flesh in sensuous lines of pleasure. When the brush dipped back into the palette, Saint felt a phantom echo, that same damp clutch as when Grey's slicked fingers dipped into his body, and his stomach sucked in tight as Grey came back with blue blended in gold to paint in crackling firebird eyes and the heart of a flickering flame burning in the creature's chest.

"Grey . . ." He could hardly get the name past his lips, his insides knotting up with a strange and confusing mix of pain, longing, guilt. It felt like a desecration to their memories, to let Grey paint over them, and yet he didn't want him to stop when they were so beautiful. When he made them live: green and blue and turquoise filling in Arturo's gecko until it was stained glass in iron blocks; soft, pale silver touched with moonlight blue on the stag that would one day be Grey's legacy on Saint's flesh. He couldn't stop his trembling. Not when every brushstroke thrilled along his skin, tingled with the cool lick of air on wetness, pulled hard at his desire and the painful way his heart beat just for Grey. Every tantalizing kiss of paint drew another hitching breath from him, and branded him with a slow-simmering need that built hotter with every moment that he held so perfectly still and let Grey use Saint's body as his canvas.

Shimmering sapphire for the coils of the dragon Philippe had left spiraling down his biceps. Remy's hummingbird on his clavicle, blooming in jewel tones until he could almost feel the living wings move with the fluttering beat of his heart. The glowing red eyes of Anubis: Victor's eyes, etched against his inner elbow and framed by the gleaming blue and gold of his headdress. One into the other into the other, until not an inch of him wasn't marked in color, not a part of his soul Grey hadn't touched.

Grey stopped, watching him with his gaze kindling, molten. "When memories become black and white," he said, "they lose all meaning. These are your memories, Saint. Let them live in color."

"You don't know what you're asking." His throat closed. "Do you know how . . . how much it *hurts* to remember them?"

Grey set the palette down, stepped closer, and gripped his hips with fingers that smeared a kaleidoscope's shades over his skin. He leaned down, resting his brow to Saint's. "Do you feel pain now?"

"Yes." Leaning hard into Grey, his heart tight, Saint closed his eyes. "Bittersweet . . . but yes."

"Do you know what a gift it is to be able to feel that? To feel anything at all?"

Saint opened his eyes, met Grey's. Hot yellow burned with such emotion, and yet there was something so remote, so inaccessible, shuttered away where, no matter what he took from Grey, Saint could never touch. Not this. This was something sacred, something not for him, and he didn't know if he should feel this ache . . . or feel relief.

"Are you saying you feel nothing?" he asked softly, and Grey reached up, touched the tip of his nose with a paint-streaked finger, traced a slow path up the bridge.

"Sometimes."

"Is now one of those times?"

"No." Grey's gaze flicked over him as his hand fell away: too searching, too penetrating, too painfully needful. "Now is one of the times when I feel too much."

When Grey kissed him, he almost pulled away. He couldn't stand how raw and stark this was. How *honest*, with the truth hovering between them until he tasted it on their lips with every slow, breath-stealing caress and flick of twining tongues. And when that taste became the salt of tears, he didn't try to stop them. He only clung harder as Grey pushed him back against the windowsill, smeared the paints between them, tangled their legs and fused their bodies and filled him with the perfect pain of knowing that this memory, this moment, would never come again. If he could have captured it in glass and held it forever, frozen time, he would have.

But time swept him away. Grey swept him away, in the slow-surging rhythm of flesh and skin and gliding touches that turned them both into a rainbow of twisting shades that changed and flowed and mixed each time they came together, seeking that perfect moment when their bodies locked and they hung in a trembling balance, on the verge, breaths held and shaking and hot.

Saint wrapped himself around Grey and held him close and shared his colors with him, as bound and blended as the fate they could never escape.

✲⋲ 32 ⋊✲

"I don't know if I can do this."

Grey sat on the edge of the table in Saint's tower, looking down at his clenched fists because he couldn't look at Saint right now. Not when he was still resonating with the echoes of last night, paint caught in little crescents under his nails, dried dashes of color that reminded him every time he'd looked at them how Saint had wept, had opened for him, had given him something indescribable that he could still feel flickering inside himself, as if it could replace the life that had been stolen away.

What Saint asked of him felt too clinical, after that. Too harsh. He felt like a surgeon getting ready to go in, with his array of tools: branches of rowan and ash, a silver candelabra, iron nails. A witch's tool kit assembled from the hardware store and the woods out back. Such simple things, but if they were right about what Saint was . . .

This would hurt him.

And Saint was asking Grey to cause him pain.

One pale arm extended, wrist up; Saint took a deep breath, his accent straining from soft, lyrical music into harsh atonal chords. "Just do it."

"Saint . . ." The words hovered on the tip of his tongue, leaving him torn, aching. Aching to ask about last night. Aching to ask if Saint had felt what he'd felt, but the lovely man flashed him a sharp look, shaking his head.

"I just want to get this over with."

"You want to suffer that much?"

"Don't I deserve it?" Saint tore his gaze away. "It's not about that. I've put this off for too long. I can't anymore. I want to know for certain. You said you'd help."

"I don't want to hurt you."

"It's not like I'm going to turn to dust. I'm not a vampire and it's not holy water." Saint clenched his fist, his arm ridging hard and tense. "Do it."

Grey nodded. He'd try the silver first, even if he was pretty sure silver was for werewolves. He tentatively pressed the candelabra against Saint's arm, ready to jerk it back immediately. Saint didn't move, didn't react, until after a moment he looked away with a grimace, blanching until he was positively green about the gills.

"How do you feel?" Grey asked.

"A little nauseated." Saint swallowed. "Nothing overwhelming. More the longer you hold it. I remember feeling this way when I picked up a silver fork, before stainless steel became more common. I just . . . I had thought . . ."

"That it was your sickness? That you were fading."

"Something like that."

He drew the candelabra back. He couldn't stand that strained, ill expression on Saint's face. "If you didn't remember anything about what you were or where you're from, why would you think otherwise? Why are you beating yourself up over this?"

"Because I should have *tried* harder. I should have tried harder to know."

"Saint." He sighed, reached for him, only to draw his hand back. When Saint's shoulders were stiff like that, he'd only pull away. "You've spent the last two hundred years in a near-perpetual state of grieving. Most people couldn't think straight after a month of that. Let alone several lifetimes."

Saint closed his eyes, worked his jaw. "I don't want forgiveness. I don't want understanding."

"Too bad. You've got them." Grey propped his hip against the table. "Even if you're immortal, you've only had the typical rules of mortal life, human physics, human skepticism. You'd have no reason to draw a correlation between touching silver and feeling vaguely ill."

"I don't even know if I feel ill." Saint stared down at his arm, at the unmarked skin. "It doesn't hurt enough. I'd feel the same way if I stood too fast. It might even be anxiety."

"Maybe there's some other way. Or maybe the mythology's wrong. As common as iron and silver are, if it were true, then humans would know about sidhe by now. Iron and silver are almost impossible to avoid. They're in everything."

"Maybe it has to get in my bloodstream, or . . ." Saint stood with a frustrated sound, his teeth bared, his eyes flashing as he swept his arm against the items on the table. "This is all pointless. It's pointless, I—"

A flash sparked with a *pop* that made Grey recoil, breathing hard. The stick of rowan wood fell onto the floor, trailing smoke, its bark singed. Wide-eyed, panting, Saint stared at the side of his hand, where a red welt had bubbled onto his skin.

Grey stared. "What . . . happened?"

"I . . . I don't . . ." Saint cradled his hand in his palm. "It's not healing," he said dully.

"What did you touch?"

"The . . . the rowan, I think."

"Have you ever touched rowan wood before?"

"No. It . . ." Saint took a deep breath, shaking his head quickly. His eyes were lost, his voice distant, remote. "It's not really common around here."

"Saint." He reached for his hand—but Saint jerked away, leaving Grey staring after him helplessly. "Does it hurt too much?"

"No . . . no, I just . . . Am I really . . .?"

No, Grey wanted to say. *No.* Because he would say anything to ease that stricken expression from Saint's face, the horror and misery in his eyes. He never should have gone along with this experiment. Not if it meant hurting him. But he couldn't lie, and finally he struggled out, "It would seem so. If sensitivity to rowan wood is any confirmation."

"Couldn't it be an . . . an allergy? Something—"

God, he didn't know how to be the voice of reason, but . . . "I don't think allergies cause smoke and sparks," he pointed out gently.

"I don't understand." Saint clutched his wounded hand against his chest. "I'm not . . . I can't do magic. I don't have any kind of powers. How can I be sidhe?"

"You're asking the wrong person. But the way you healed before . . . that's a power, isn't it?"

"Yeah. I . . . Yeah." Saint turned his back to him, his shoulders slumping, his head bowed. "I need a minute."

"Saint—"

He reached for Saint's shoulder—wanting, *needing* to hold him, to offer some kind of comfort, the shelter of that closeness they'd shared the night before—but Saint knocked his hand away fiercely, turning on him with a snarl.

"*Just get out*! I don't want to see you. Can't you get that through your head?"

"Saint—"

"What?" Those soft pink lips he'd kissed a hundred times thinned into an unforgiving line. "Do you think you'll make me feel better? Do you think because now the monster has a name, it'll be okay? You—you can't even *understand*. You're human. What the hell do you know?"

Grey stilled. Hurt welled inside him like something had broken and spilled, pouring out its contents heavily inside his chest. Right. What the hell did he know about the pain of isolation? What did he know about spending his entire life wondering what was wrong with him, but fearing to look the answers dead in the eye?

He was only *human*, after all.

This had been a terrible fucking idea. This entire experiment. He'd only wanted to help Saint, so that once Grey was gone Saint might, just *might* be closer to finding some kind of understanding. Some kind of peace. An end to his pain. But all this had done was create more, anguish brimming so clearly behind the fury hardening Saint's features into a mask that denied the intimacy Grey still burned to reclaim.

He didn't want to go. He didn't want to leave, when Saint was hurting. But Bondye damn him, he wouldn't force himself on the other man. Saint didn't want him here.

He swallowed back the hard constriction in his throat, turned away from that furious gaze, and walked out.

✳ 33 ✳

I, Saint thought, *am such a fucking asshole.*

Nuo had practically shoved him out of the ambulance at the end of their shift, telling him to go get drunk or get fucked or do whatever it took to stop being such a surly ass and driving her crazy for the second night in a row. Even their patients had noticed. The old woman they'd picked up from the retirement home, her fractured hip in a temporary cast, had propped herself on her elbows and watched him with her brown eyes shrewd and snapping, her lips pursed.

Boy, if you were mine, I'd tell you to fetch the switch, 'cause I ain't here for your lip.

I'm sorry, ma'am. I'm sorry.

Why was it so much easier to apologize to a stranger than it was to Grey?

He stood outside the coffee shop where he'd first taken Grey, and willed himself to go inside. Because he had nowhere else to go. Because his tower still smelled like burning rowan wood and singed flesh, and it made him ill. In just a few short weeks he'd gotten so used to finishing his shift and going back to Grey's place, to watching him paint until his body moved like music and hypnotized Saint for hours that culminated so breathlessly in Grey's mouth on his throat and Grey's cock surging hard inside him and that perfect feeling when Saint broke and clenched tight enough to imprint every inch of Grey's shape from the inside.

But he'd told Grey to get out. He'd chased him out, and since then there'd been not one phone call, no sign of that ratty truck trundling to the hospital to drag him off until he stopped pushing Grey away. Because he'd fucked up. He'd fucked up—and this time Grey wasn't going to come to him, wasn't going to do the work for him after the way Saint had lashed out, discarding him when he had so little of him to start with.

Saint was just supposed to kill him. Not hurt him, tear him open, eviscerate him with the blade of Saint's sharpened tongue.

Fuck. At least a few cups of coffee and a slice of pie would take his mind off this, and keep him from going home to that tower that had never seemed quite so empty as it did now.

What do you care for emptiness? You're a leanan sidhe.

A monster.

You don't belong around other people.

The bell above the door tinkled as he stepped inside. The woman behind the counter glanced up, brushing a few strands of her russet hair from her face. He didn't like her. He hadn't liked her since he'd come here with Grey and she'd watched them like she was waiting to stand judgment—and he liked her even less when she smirked and spoke.

"Here again?"

"I didn't know a repeat customer was so rare," Saint bit off, and slid onto a stool at the counter. "Though your coffee's pretty shit. I shouldn't be surprised."

She grinned, slid an empty cup down in front of him, and poured: thick, black, steaming, probably bitter sludge no matter how much sugar he put into it. "Blame the owner, not me." A menu dropped onto the counter next to the cup, but her gaze was on him, pale green eyes watching him, narrowed, thoughtful. "You work right around the corner, but you never come in here. I know all the other EMTs and half the nurses by name. But not you."

Saint arched a brow, then tapped the name tag still pinned to his uniform jacket: *Xav*. She snorted.

"Oh, aye. I get that." Her own name tag read *Guineveve*, and she tweaked it wryly. "But I think you're lying."

He bristled. "About what?"

"That's for you to tell, isn't it?" She tilted her head, then shrugged a little too offhandedly. "But I remember last time, you were here with that painter bloke. Famous one, ain't he?"

He closed his eyes, trying to ignore the aching clutch in his chest, but it wouldn't go away. He'd come here to avoid thinking about Grey, not to have him thrown in his face.

"And I'm not this time," he ground out, and willed her to drop it.

Her silence was more telling than the soft words that followed. "But you want to be."

He glared. "What the fuck business is it of yours?"

"Testy," she lilted mockingly. "When you have so little time, do you really want to waste a minute of it?"

"What?" Saint's stomach bottomed out; he half rose off his stool. He stared at her, but she was already walking away, picking up a rag and shaking it out. "How do you know—"

She flicked him a mild glance. "Know what?"

He couldn't breathe. What had he been thinking? That she knew what he was, what he'd done, what he would continue to do until he couldn't stand living like this over the eons? No. No, and if he told her, she'd think he was crazy. She was just a bored café employee entertaining herself by poking at one clearly miserable man, and he'd come close to spilling out his heart just because he desperately needed to not be alone with this anymore.

But you weren't alone with it.

You had Grey.

Staying away from him won't keep him alive, Saint. You did this. Own it. No matter what happens, he's fucked . . . and so are you.

He closed his eyes and curled his hands around the coffee cup, but its heat did nothing to warm the chill in his heart. "Nothing. Nothing. Never mind."

Do you suddenly think you can save him, Saint?

As if he could save anyone, when he couldn't even save himself.

You aren't saving him, you selfish prick.

You're just leaving him to die alone.

✳⚬ 34 ⚬✳

He couldn't paint.

And he didn't think it was because he was missing his muse, either. This wasn't some fucking metaphysical mumbo jumbo. This was his head and his heart having a stupid fight, and his inspiration getting pulled in a tug-of-war in between.

Just . . . go to him.

Swallow his pride. Swallow how much it had hurt when Saint smacked his hand away. He shouldn't be fucking pining like this after three damned days, anyway. That wasn't healthy. That was some kind of fixation, obsession, as if he could boil this symbiotic strangeness down to a codependent relationship and write it off as that. If only it were so simple. If only he could say, *We just need some space and we'll be fine,* when space might well end up killing them both.

Maybe he was afraid of being alone with his thoughts. Alone with that dark channel of nothingness that funneled everything in his mind toward the one inevitable conclusion: *It's your fault.*

The voice in his head, the one that whispered his feelings away and blanketed them in silence.

Everything is always your fault, Grey.

You hurt Saint. You burned him. And now he's never coming back, because he hates you.

He knew that voice lied. He knew it amplified everything he hated and made it more real, but it made him afraid, too. Afraid that it was right, and if he didn't swallow everything he felt and admit to being wrong, forget his own hurt . . . Saint would never come back. Grey would just . . . die here, meaningless and alone, without the will to even paint. He could feel it happening, his skin shriveling and tight and dry. Apparently absence didn't slow the process. It only made him worry that whatever he'd lost was bleeding away into the ether, useless and wasted, without Saint there to absorb it like a flower taking in the sun.

He didn't know what to do. And that voice held him paralyzed, turning in circles, unable to choose one course or the other, stuck in a limbo that had become so familiar that it felt like home.

He sank to his knees before the veve against the wall and lit the candles one by one.

"Erzulie," he whispered and closed his eyes, crossed himself. "Tell me what to do. Tell me this is right. Let me hear you in the wind, the way I once did; let me feel your presence in my soul. Save me. Deliver me. Deliver me from . . . from . . ."

life
pain
doubt
emptiness
sorrow
loneliness

He opened his eyes, reaching out to touch the lines he'd hand-stitched in the altar cloth with such loving care.

"Deliver me from myself."

There was no answer. The loa never answered directly. Sometimes he thought they never answered at all, and faith was nothing but seeing a correlation between what would eventually happen anyway and the slow and patient hand of the gods.

But sometimes, he just . . . needed to believe.

Or he would have nothing else.

The security buzzer on his intercom rattled over the apartment. He lifted his head, frowning, rose to his feet—and swayed as his knees buckled beneath him. He caught the wall, closed his eyes, and waited for the dizzy spell to pass, then moved to the window. Slowly, so slowly, his body more of a sluggish and disobedient thing with every day, he leaned hard against the sill and bent over to see who was waiting at the building's door. The last unanswered message from his agent had involved, among other things, a threat to show up with a leash to drag him out if he didn't fucking *pick up*, and he didn't quite trust her not to make good on that. He half expected to see her standing outside with a collar and a chain and a riding crop for good measure.

He didn't expect to see Saint.

Saint stood below as if Erzulie had delivered him to Grey's doorstep, looking up, his eyes wide and almost pleading. Grey's breaths hitched. His heart turned over.

Saint had come to him.

Please, Saint mouthed, resting a hand next to the building's door. *Please.*

Grey thrust away from the window, ignoring the creaking ache in his bones and stumbling toward the elevator to buzz Saint up. He felt like his heart could beat again, all of a sudden. Like his lungs remembered how to breathe. And the groaning elevator moved too slowly, too fucking grindingly creakingly *slowly*, while he hovered near the gate and waited for it to fall down and spill Saint out into his apartment.

For a moment they stared at each other. No words between them. Grey didn't even know where to start. But he tried.

"Saint—"

I missed you, he'd wanted to say, but Saint shook his head.

"Don't," he pleaded softly. "Let me just . . . say this. Please."

Grey faltered.

He's come to tell you he's through, that voice said. *That you weren't even worth saving that night in the ambulance. That this deal of yours is over and done. It's been fun, but it's really not convenient anymore.*

He nodded, bracing himself. Saint's lashes trembled, and he scrubbed his palms on his thighs.

"I . . ." He stopped, teeth clacking together audibly, and breathed in deep. Words tumbled out of him in a rush so fast Grey could barely follow, yet he hung on every one. "I'm sorry. I'm *sorry*. I'm scared, and it makes me horrible and cruel. I don't . . . I don't want to be a *thing*. Something that was never human. And I don't want to cross this horrible bridge where I can never turn back, by *choosing* to do this to you. And I wanted to blame it on you, the proof of what I am. Even more, I wanted to push you away because if I didn't feel this, if I didn't care, if I could just let it be a *transaction*, maybe you'd stop dying. But it doesn't work that way, and I . . ." He shook his head, started forward, stopped. "It's not a transaction. And I'm *scared*, Grey. Of myself . . . Of losing you."

He just doesn't want to die, the voice in his head said, cynical and cold.

Grey ignored it.

Grey ignored it and closed the distance between them to pull Saint close, to wrap him in his arms and feel that warmth he'd been missing for days. To savor that raw honesty that was so unlike the coy, smirking man who'd tried to lure him in but only trapped him when he'd shown Grey the hurting, wounded, beautiful reality underneath. He kissed Saint's hair, then buried his face in it and held him as tight as he could.

"It's all right," he whispered. "It's all right to be afraid. Just don't push me away, Saint. Please don't. While this is happening, I can't stand to miss you."

"I know. I know, I'm sorry . . ."

"Stop apologizing."

Grey kissed him, suddenly needing him as if he'd held himself pent up for days and couldn't keep it inside anymore. He tortured them both with little tastes, soft brushes, never letting himself delve deeper until Saint fisted slender hands in his shirt, dragged him down, sealed their mouths together with an answering longing that Grey needed right now, wordless affirmation that this was Saint's choice. That they were in this together, until the blessed end.

Erzulie, thank you, he thought, as he nudged Saint toward a bed that had missed his heat for far too many hours.

Slim fingers gripped his hips, shaped him like a work of art, drew him close until his back arched and his blood burned. Saint tumbled onto the bed and drew Grey with him, twining them together until they fit just right, and Grey shivered at the taut quiver of that graceful body against his own.

Saint looked up at him, his eyes clear and bright and sheened so damp. He touched trembling fingertips to Grey's equally trembling lips.

"Use me," Saint said.

But as Grey leaned down to claim his lips once more, he ached inside.

Use me, Saint had said.

But what Grey had wanted to hear, more than anything . . . was *Love me*.

✳ 35 ✳

Saint curled in the dark with Grey's arm heavy over his waist, and tried to pretend he couldn't hear or feel the coughing. The bone-deep, rib-rattling coughs that made Grey's entire body shake against him. The coughs that were his fault. How was he supposed to be okay with this when Grey was dying second by second in his arms right now, every exhalation a drop of his life that Saint sucked into his own lungs?

He stroked his fingers over Grey's scalp as if that could soothe him, but in the end nothing he did could make this better. It was too late for that. It had been too late since that first kiss.

"I'm sorry." He rubbed his cheek to the tight, soft nap of Grey's hair. "I'm sorry it hurts."

"It's all right." Another cough before Grey subsided, pillowing his cheek to Saint's chest. "I knew it would."

"Is it your loa that give you such calm? Such acceptance?"

"Perhaps. Or maybe it's just you."

"It can't be me."

"I told you—you don't get to decide what I like. You don't get to decide what I accept, either. What brings me peace is my choice." Grey chuckled and rested his chin on Saint's chest, looking up at him. "I think I love you. That alone calms my heart."

Yet it only stirred a storm in Saint's—a sudden crash, washing over him and dragging him under until he couldn't breathe. "Don't," he choked. "Don't say that."

Grey watched him with steady, unshakable certainty. "I can't lie about it."

"But you can't—"

You can't love me for what I really am and mean it.

No one else ever has.

He backed himself against the headboard, retreating so quickly Grey tumbled against the sheets. "How do you know it's even real? How do you know it's not just . . . just some spell I've woven over you without meaning to?"

"You have." Grey pushed himself up and cupped his cheek. "But it's not because of what you are. It's because of *who* you are, Saint." His voice softened. "My Saint."

"Grey . . . Grey, *no*. Loving me won't save you."

"I never thought it could. That's not the nature of this thing." Grey shifted to settle against the headboard next to him, and gathered him into his arms until he couldn't escape—not Grey's warmth, not the feeling of each low word rumbling through his chest. "I never went into this expecting to be saved. I never thought love could change my life and make me want to live. That's not how it works. Love can sometimes give you someone to support you while you look for a way out of the dark . . . but it can't heal anyone. Love only cures everything in fairy tales."

"Love's just a weapon." He buried his face against Grey's chest and squeezed his eyes shut. "That's the real world. No fairy tale. Love is only good for hurting people."

"Does my love hurt you?"

"Don't ask me that."

He shoved away, but Grey refused to let go, though where he found the strength when the once-strong muscles hung lax on his bones, Saint didn't know. He froze, terrified of hurting him, but Grey only smiled and reached up to tuck his hair back.

"Don't pull away. You don't have to love me. It'll be easier for you if you don't. Just don't pull away from me." He coaxed Saint down to rest his head to Grey's chest again. "I'm just a silly mortal, after all. I can't help myself."

"Shut up. Just shut up, stupid."

Grey chuckled. "As you wish."

Saint curled closer and reminded himself to *breathe* until the urge to hyperventilate passed. The urge to run, like a criminal fleeing the scene of a homicide. That's what this was, in the end. Murder. And the fact that Grey loved him made it worse, so much worse. Something rose up his throat; something that tried to be a sob, until he swallowed it into a hiccup.

"I wasn't meant for this," he rasped. "I wasn't meant to be a killer. I can't believe that. That I did something so horrible before I lost my memory that it doomed me to this."

Grey stroked his arm, slow and soothing. "Is that why you do what you do? Being an EMT."

"Yeah." He managed a rough laugh, but god, he needed to move on, to talk about anything else but Grey's damning *love*. "That, and it's easier to pass certification with a hundred-year-old medical education."

"So you don't have any actual medical training?"

"Nothing formal since . . . oh . . . nineteen twenty-three, except one EMT course. I forged the certs for the rest."

A smirk curved Grey's lips. "That's comforting."

"You'd scream if you had any idea how little medical technology has changed since then."

"You're avoiding the subject."

"Mngh . . . stop knowing me." He sighed, *thunking* his brow to Grey's shoulder. "I take lives. Shouldn't I at least try to save them when I can?"

"Are you trying to pay off your karmic debt?"

"Maybe." His chest felt like it was trying to crack open. "Or maybe I'm hoping if I see enough people die on that stretcher . . . it'll stop hurting so much. Or maybe it'll hurt too much and I'll finally just . . . wander off alone into the woods and never come back."

"How do you stand it?"

"Stand what?"

"Being so alone, when you're afraid anyone you get close to will die."

"I *can't* stand it." Shame flushed through him. "I'm weak. And I keep telling myself it won't happen again, but it does. Because I can't stand to be alone anymore, and my willpower crumbles. And I tell myself if I just hope hard enough, this one time . . . he won't die."

In Grey's silence, in that tight hold, were a million things unsaid. *I love you. I need you. I want you. I'll die for you, Saint.*

But more than anything, his silence said, *I'm listening*—and so Saint tried. He tried so very hard to just . . . *speak*, and let out all the things he'd walled inside.

"I keep asking myself . . ." His throat clotted, but he forced words past, even if each one felt as large as a fist inside his throat. "What was wrong with me? I feel like someone threw me away, Grey. I had to have been someone before this. Human, sidhe, either way . . . I was *someone*. I had to have known people. Didn't I have family? Friends? Anyone who would look for me?" His eyes stung, burned, blurred. "Or did someone just use me up and throw me away?"

"If they did, it was their loss. You have people now. Nuo." A soft kiss, a vow, a promise. "Me."

But that promise is a lie, Saint thought.

"I don't have you for long, do I?"

Grey didn't answer. Saint hadn't expected him to.

Nothing either of them said could change what they'd done.

❈❦ 36 ❧❈

Grey didn't remember falling asleep. It was like that too often lately; his body just gave out on him, dragged him down until he could endure consciousness again. He needed to rest more and more, sleeping until it no longer hurt so much to even stand up, let alone hold a brush. The only time he didn't feel the pain was when he was painting and that fire ate him hollow again, and when he slept.

But he woke to a pervasive soreness, the umber glow of afternoon light, and the sound of cloth on cloth. Saint, twisting carefully out of his arms and reaching for his clothing. Grey stretched one arm across the sheets to trace a fingertip over his hip.

"Where are you going?"

"Work." Saint leaned over and brushed a faint taste of honey to his lips with a kiss, then pulled away. "As much as I missed you, people are still out there falling off ladders and having head-on collisions with trees."

He grinned. "You're actually admitting you missed me?"

"Try not to be too smug about it." Saint stepped into his pants, hoisting them around his hips, and gave Grey an uncertain look. "Will you be all right alone?"

"I'm not on a walker yet." He pushed himself up and draped an arm over his knee. "I'll know who to call if I need 911."

"That's not funny, Grey."

"I'm sorry." He sighed. "I can't help but laugh about it. When something's been a part of you this long . . ."

"When *what's* been a part of you?" Saint sank down on the bed again. He pleaded, his accent throaty and sweet, begging. "Grey, why can't you just *tell* me what's driving this?"

"Why do you keep asking? Do you think if I tell you, you can somehow magically fix me?"

"No. I can't fix you. You said it yourself: no one can fix you but yourself, if you're even broken." A soft hand curled over his, squeezing gently. "I'm asking so I'll know you as you truly are. So that when you become a part of me, I'll remember you in everything you were. More than just a name. Names are easily forgotten." Saint leaned closer. "I don't want to forget you, Grey."

Grey looked down at their twined hands. White on black, moon and night, sun and shadow. His chest seized tight. "I hate to disappoint you, then," he whispered, each word like swallowing thorns. "Because I don't really have a reason."

"No?"

"No."

Grey lifted his gaze to Saint's, and told himself to just . . .

Tell the truth.

He'd only wanted Saint more for the truth of him, the reality underneath the mask. He had to trust Saint would feel the same, and wouldn't pull away.

"That's the ugly part of it," he said. "If you ask me why, if you're looking for some terrible traumatic event that pushed me over the edge, there's nothing. Just every slow day chipping away at me, eroding until it becomes a landslide that buries me. That's how it works."

Saint's brow wrinkled. "How what works?"

He wet his lips. Made himself say it. The word that felt like a scarlet letter and a crushing weight in one, that said, *Broken, so broken, and no one will ever understand because they think you're just* sad, *this melodramatic artist who needs to get over himself.*

"Depression," he said, and waited for the ax to drop.

But there was only Saint's weight easing further onto the bed—then pressing close into his side. Saint's arms wrapping around one of his and hugging it to his chest. Saint's head on his shoulder. *Saint*, period, there and not walking away.

"Tell me about it," Saint said.

"It's . . . hard to explain." He struggled a moment, before continuing, "Nothing's wrong and everything's wrong. You don't have the energy for the things you love, or when you do it comes in short bursts that you grasp on to before it's gone again and it takes everything in you just to pick yourself up off the floor. And you hate yourself for not having a reason for it, because other people would expect a reason, but it's just . . . there. It just *is*. And sooner or later that voice that tells you there's no point in trying, there's no point in feeling, there's no point in getting up . . . starts to say there's no point in waking up. That there's no point in living." His gut was made of knots, snaring around each other. "That voice is really persuasive, Saint. And I'm sick of hearing it. If I die, it'll be quiet. And I won't be counting the days left until I'm gone anyway, and nothing I've done will have mattered."

"Grey." Saint said his name like a benediction, and coaxed him closer. "Grey, come here."

He leaned hard into Saint. Buried his face in his shoulder and for just a few moments, let himself be weak. He shook, and not even clutching hard at the lovely man in his arms could make it stop.

"I'm sorry," he whispered. "You must think I'm so broken."

"No," Saint murmured against his ear, warm and sweet. "I think you're human."

"If I die this way, at least it will matter. At least it will mean something for you."

"Don't. Please don't say that."

"You're giving me what I want. Don't hate yourself for what you are, when it's what I want." He rubbed his cheek to Saint's shoulder. "*You're* what I want."

And for a moment, just a moment, he wondered what it would be like to wake up to this every day. To know that on the other side of the dark this was waiting for him, if he could find the strength to fight his way back.

But he didn't think he could. Not anymore.

"I've tried meds," he said, speaking almost too quickly. He suddenly needed Saint to know he wasn't just . . . rolling over, giving up, doing nothing. "I did. They had so many adverse effects they almost made me suicidal on their own. And therapy . . . the words blend together after a while. I hate the tone of voice they use. They talk to me like I'm crazy. And it makes me feel crazy. That voice feels like they don't want to get too invested in you, because who knows when you'll be gone." He exhaled heavily, holding back a tired laugh. "EMTs have it, too."

Saint made a considering sound. "Did I?"

"No. You spoke to me like you were angry, and I wondered why."

"I'm not angry. Not now."

"No?" Grey smiled and held Saint as long as he could, for as long as Saint would let him. "Then I'm glad."

"Yeah," Saint said, and nestled into his shoulder. "Me too."

Yet even as he leaned against him, even as he held him close and took every moment for what it was worth . . .

Grey wondered what Saint wasn't saying, when the silence fell between them like the calm before the storm.

37

Go to him.

Saint stood outside the gates of the Bonaventure Cemetery. The night was moonless, and the statues and crosses and gravestones were just formless white blurs, specters in the dark. He should go back to Grey, he told himself. He'd finished work almost an hour ago, and he didn't need to be out here in the predawn gloom, catching dew on his eyelashes and staring through the gateway into the world of the dead.

Yet he couldn't help himself. He stepped underneath the moss-festooned archways, the low-hanging branches of trees, and made his way among the plots by a route so familiar it was a miracle he hadn't embedded his footprints permanently into the earth. He passed the newer markers, with their perfect laser-cut engraving; passed the more worn ones, that had been here fifty years or more. Deeper, into the corners of the cemetery where the graves were so old no one knew who they belonged to anymore.

Except Saint.

He stopped before a battered lump of granite, every striation in its color committed to memory. The name on the headstone was long worn off, the marker left smooth and irregular and little more than a stone outcropping. He sank into a crouch and brushed a bit of leaf debris from the top, then pressed his hand over where the engraving used to be.

"Hello, Calen," he whispered. "What would you think if you could see me now?"

Calen didn't answer. Calen never answered.

But still it brought Saint comfort to feel the weathered granite against his palm, familiar as his own fingerprints and just as indelible.

"I thought it would be here," a soft voice said, and Saint whirled, rising to his feet so swiftly he nearly tumbled over Calen's tombstone.

Guineveve stood on the dirt path, so simple and ordinary with her uniform shucked, her hands tucked into the pockets of her hoodie, her russet hair loosed around her face. Her smile was pleasant but her eyes were strange, unsettling, something lighting the pale green that made Saint back away, watching her warily.

"How did you find me?"

"I found you because this is where I would be, in your situation." She smiled faintly. "Where I've been several times before."

"My situation?"

"Let's not dissemble anymore." She stepped closer. "You know what you are. You know what *I* am. You feel it. We're kin, boy. Or did you think shit coffee was the only thing warding you away?"

Shock punched the air out of him. "Kin . . .? You— I— What?"

"Not that way. No." She pulled a hand from her hoodie pocket and held it up. "I'm sorry if I spoke carelessly. Hurtfully. I'm not . . . whomever left you behind." She smiled sadly. "But someone left me too. Someone I can't remember, no more than I can remember anything else. I am what you are. Though if I'm right . . . I've been at it far longer than you have."

"You've known? A-all this time, you've known . . .?"

"I knew the first day you came in. And I knew what was happening between you and your fellow." She studied him closely. "Hurts more this time, doesn't it?"

"Don't. Don't, you don't get to—"

"To understand?"

"I don't *know*!" He sucked in ragged, stabbing gasps of air. "What do you want from me? Why are you telling me this? What the hell are you thinking, coming at me with this out of nowhere? Do you think knowing there are more of us out there killing people will help?"

"It helped me. To know I'm not alone in this curse."

"*Curse.* So it is a curse."

She shrugged. "If you want to see it that way. I try not to. But I didn't come here to upset you, boy. I came to help."

His upper lip curled. He took another step back, until his calves hit Calen's headstone. "You can't help me."

"I can tell you how to save your Grey. But you won't like the easy way." She chuckled, brief and humorless. "Even if it's not all that easy."

"*Tell me.*"

"The only way to break a leanan sidhe's hold is to find someone else to take the victim's place."

He stared at her numbly, while the words tumbled through his brain but refused to click together in a way that made sense. This wasn't real. Was this how Grey had felt when Saint tried to explain? This sudden shift in the patterns of the world, reconfiguring into something new that he didn't know how to interpret. It was too abrupt, blindsiding him. He'd seen it happen to a hundred, a thousand humans, people who lay on his stretcher and whimpered in pain and tried to cope with the fact that life had simply *happened*, and just like a speeding car or a lone gunman or a lightning strike, sometimes things crashed into you before you were ready to deal.

He couldn't face this. He turned away, staring down at the headstone instead of into those calm, mocking green eyes. "That's not an answer. That's not acceptable. It's still someone dying."

"But it's not the one you love."

"*I don't love him!*"

"Don't you?" She moved to stand at his side, looking down at the unmarked grave. "It doesn't work if you don't love them. They don't give you what you need. But here you are, bright and brimming with the flush of life."

"*I don't love him.* Why should I? It's all this playact, going through the motions. Pretending at love." Even as he said them, the words tasted bitter, raw in his throat. "Everything he feels toward me is because of what I am."

"What makes you think that?"

Because no one could truly love me for the murderer I am, he thought, but said aloud, "How he acts about me. This . . . entire affliction."

"Why couldn't that be genuine attraction?"

"Why would it be?"

"Why wouldn't it be?" Her glance was almost pitying. "We have no more power to bewitch men and women than they give us. If they fall under our spell, it's because they see something in us they genuinely desire. Something they want so much they can't help themselves." She sighed. "All this time you've been thinking he only wants you because of some kind of fae magic?"

"Y-yes." Saint's fingers curled into fists, biting into his palms. That was somehow worse, that Grey could really love him. That he was killing himself to love him. "And . . . because I can give him what he wants. That's all I am to him. All I've ever been to anyone. Something to use. Some want art, some want beauty; he wants death, and he's fading already. He's so close to gone, and I . . ."

"That upsets you."

"Of *course* it upsets me!" he flared, struggling not to scream, to sob, ending up snarling. "What kind of monster do you think I am?"

But she only smiled, and brushed her fingers against his arm. "I never thought you were a monster at all."

"But I am," he whispered dully. Beneath his feet Calen was just bones and dust, nothing left of that smile, nothing left of him but the marks on Saint's skin. "I tried to be a monster. I tried not to care. I thought if I could just be shatterproof, if I could keep from letting this break me . . . I could live without this ripping me open every time."

"Child." She clucked her tongue. "None of us, human or sidhe, are shatterproof. We break because it's in our nature to break. It just means we have to put ourselves back together stronger next time."

"And if I can't?"

She fixed him with a long, measuring look. "You can."

"I have no reason left to. Everything was taken from me. Who I was, what I was . . . and now I'm going to lose him. I used to think I could fill the spaces with *them*, but all it does is leave me more empty every time. And after him . . . I'll just . . . be nothing. Nothing at all but memories of everyone but myself."

"Why do you see this as a loss? What if it was something you were given? What if this is a *gift*?" she asked. "How often does anyone get a chance to start over with a clean slate?"

"So I shouldn't even *try* to remember?"

"If what you forgot made you what you are . . . Do you really think it's worth remembering?"

Her gaze held him, green as spring leaves, and he suddenly thought: *I know you. I don't know how, but I know you.*

He stepped closer, reaching out, then pulled back. "Who are you, really?"

She smiled—a strange, sad smile that was too much like looking in a mirror. "Every road has been walked at least once, often by those far older than you."

"That's not an answer."

"Isn't it?"

"*Please.* I need to know."

"No, you don't," she murmured. "Love what you have. Not what you lost."

"But I'm going to lose it all over again."

"Are you?"

"I'm *killing* him."

"There are other ways."

"Sacrificing someone else. As if that's any better. A life is a life. Even if one doesn't belong to someone I . . . I . . ."

Guineveve made a sympathetic sound. "You can't say it, can you?"

"No." He sank to one knee and stroked the smooth-worn edges of Calen's headstone. "It feels like a nail in his coffin."

They remained there in silence for some time, until her hand fell to rest on his shoulder. "I should go."

He looked up at her. Again that sense of familiarity, of *knowing*, eluding just out of his reach. "May . . . I come by the shop to see you tomorrow?"

"Sea." She pronounced it like *shaa*, lilting and throaty, and something inside him sparked. She watched him keenly. "You recognize that, don't you?"

"You . . . said yes. That means yes, doesn't it?"

"Sea." She smiled. "There may be some Gaelic in you yet."

"Guineveve?"

"Hm?"

"How many others are there?"

"Others?"

"Like us."

"I don't know." Her lips pursed. "I've only met four others, in all my time. We pass so easily for human that sometimes we might brush against each other and never know. Two ships passing in the night, as they say. We're just ordinary people, child. Not that different from anyone else."

"How did you know me, then?"

"I know that look."

"What look?"

"When it gets to be too much to bear. I had that look once, myself."

He closed his eyes. *That* look. The one that haunted him when he stared in the mirror. When his own reflection saw him so coldly, and in his own eyes he saw the word *murderer*, accusing and dark.

"How did you get rid of it?" he whispered.

"I didn't. I just learned to hide it better."

"Should I?"

"No." She covered his hand, trapping it against the tombstone, and squeezed it for just a moment. "Feel everything as much as you can, as beautifully as you can, for as long as you can."

"If I can't?"

If there's nothing beautiful left inside me?

She looked down at him, searching him as if searching for some sign. Prying him apart. Weighing him. Judging him on some scale he couldn't understand, couldn't even see.

"You can," she said, and then she left him.

Alone with the dead, and alone with his endless thoughts.

⦓ 38 ⦔

He was painting again when he heard the creak of the elevator and the sound of Saint's bag hitting the floor. Grey thought this might be his last work. The brush trembled in his hand, and not even the fire could hold him steady enough to make the lines run straight.

He didn't know what he was painting, anyway. It wasn't Bawon Samedi, though he saw his face everywhere. Wasn't Maman Brigitte. This was someone in moon-silver blue and glowing heart's-blood pink, all soft warm flowing lines. She tried to talk to him through the canvas, but he was too tired to listen—and he didn't think he could let go, until he knew her.

But when Saint stepped in, he set the brush down with one last curious glance for the canvas before crossing the room to gather Saint's drooping shoulders close.

"You're late," he said, and kissed his jaw. "Rough night?"

Saint leaned into him hard. So hard it almost pushed him over, even though he didn't want to admit the weakness. "Something like that."

"What happened?"

"Nothing. I've just been . . . thinking. Wondering. Why they had to die." There was something so dejected in Saint's voice, something Grey had never heard before and yet recognized at a visceral level. "Maybe they just died because I wasn't enough for them to live for. Because they were just using me. Maybe . . . maybe all we are is what others can use us for."

"Come here."

He guided Saint to the couch, sank down with him, curled him in his arms until he made a tight, trembling bundle that Grey only wished he could shelter more. He rested his chin to the top of his head, and murmured into his hair.

"I don't believe that. And I don't believe you weren't enough. You're more than enough for anyone. For me." He held him tighter, as if where his words fell short, his arms could suffice. "Fuck, you're too much. I *need* you, Saint. I couldn't care less about the paintings. But needing you has nothing to do with my life, or its end. You can't make that choice for me. No one should live or die for someone else."

"But you're dying for me," Saint whispered miserably.

"I'm dying for me." He closed his eyes and nuzzled into Saint's hair. "We were just lucky enough to find each other. Lucky enough that if I'm to give my life, it can be for yours."

Saint pulled away, leaving him cold, and looked up at him with something stark and hurting in his eyes. "Grey, I—"

"What is it?"

"Nothing. It's nothing." Saint shook his head with a sound that meant *It's everything.* "I'm going to go take a shower."

Grey watched him go. He could push, he could pry, but then they'd only go to bed angry, and still Saint would have told him nothing. He knew his ways by now. Knew when to press, when not to. And now was one of those times when he knew to let it go, even if he worried for whatever had sent Saint's thoughts down this path.

But still, he wondered: *What are you hiding from me, Saint?*

✳ 39 ✳

Another day. Another careful deflection. And alone in his tower, Saint stared at the tape recorder and tried to make himself speak. The last words he'd said still left their disgusting residue on his tongue, lies to put distance between himself and Grey.

Sorry. I have to be in early. Nuo needs me to help her with duplicating and logging a problem with the ambulance. There's something wrong with the . . . I don't even know. She said something about the dash.

When what he'd really meant was, *I don't know how to tell you this, and I need a little space.*

He pressed Record, but the only thing it was picking up was his ragged breaths.

"I . . ."

Talk. *Talk.* This was supposed to help him figure out who he was, but Guinevere made him wonder if there was any point.

"I met someone. She says she's like me. That we're the same. That I . . . I'm not *alone.*" Admitting that felt like a crime, like he should be judged for the quiet relief at knowing he wasn't the only one. Knowing that Guinevere had survived this for longer than he had. "She told me there may be a way to save him. To save Grey. But the cost, if he doesn't want to be saved . . ."

Numbers ticked by, adding more seconds to the eternity of his life. If he thought back hard, he could tally every second in the billions, trillions, septillions. What difference did these seconds make?

"This is still so pointless," he said, and threw the recorder down without bothering to turn it off. "What am I recording, other than a confession to murder?"

✳❡ 40 ❧✳

Guinevere was behind the counter again, when he ducked into the shop. She looked paler today, the shadows of her eyelids just a little bluer, and Saint hated that he understood.

She was holding out, too. Waiting as long as she could, but she wouldn't be able to wait much longer.

She was already slinging out a fresh cup of coffee swill before he finished sitting down, a stack of sugars next to the mug. He wondered if she shared his sweet tooth. If that was true, about the stories—that fae loved milk and honey and candied, sugared things.

"You're brooding," she said, propping her elbows on the counter.

He wrinkled his nose. "I don't know how to tell him."

"Tell him what?"

"That he doesn't have to die. Does it matter, when he *wants* to die?"

"Don't know. If he wants to die, why are you worried?" When he didn't answer, she sighed. "Because you love him. Enough to sacrifice yourself for him?"

"If I do . . . won't it be the same? Just a few more cold weeks and then I'll die, instead of him."

"I told you . . . someone has to take his place."

"What happens if it's me?" He looked down, toying with a sugar packet. "What if I choose to take his place?"

"Then you'll die." She shrugged. "Eventually."

Her tone caught him, and he squinted at her. "There's something you aren't telling me."

"You're a smart boy," she said offhandedly. "You'll figure it out."

"Don't play games. I need your help. I don't know how to figure this out by myself. I don't know how to *be* this thing, not for two hundred years of trying."

"Did you ever think about simply . . . becoming human?"

He rocked back on his stool, staring at her. The idea that he even *could* struck a hard, ferocious blow that felt like it had gutted him. Despair, hope, doubt: he didn't know which to feel, and so all three caught him up hard and squeezed him tight.

"How?" he asked breathlessly. "How can I?"

She looked over her shoulder, then swept a glance around the restaurant before leaning closer, dropping her voice. "Leanan sidhe cannot kill leanan sidhe. And from the look of you, I'd say you've guessed you can't kill yourself. But take his place? Ah, that's a different story." She hummed under her breath. "The geas breaks. Both yours and his. You'll live a mortal life, but so will he. You give back what you took from him, until the balance evens out."

"How do you know that?"

"Stories, passed by those I've met. Saw it happen once."

"Then it's true?"

"Wouldn't taste so bitter if it weren't."

"He'll recover. And I . . . I'll age like a human." The words didn't feel real. His blood ran too thin, his veins constricting, his entire body seeming to contract on itself. "Die like a human."

"Does that terrify you?"

"*Yes*," he said, and felt it down to his wavering bones. "But . . . no."

Dying—in forty years, fifty, sixty, seventy—was frightening. But it happened to everyone. And if he died naturally, after a life where he no longer had to hide, to pretend, to kill . . .

Wasn't that worth facing the fears that every other human on this earth knew so intimately?

Especially if it meant Grey would *live*?

Guineveve straightened, and pulled a wrapped slice of lemon meringue pie from under the counter. She stripped the Saran Wrap away, and slid it in front of him. "Think about it while you eat your pie. Nothing says you have to choose now."

But I don't have much time to choose at all.

Not when Grey was nothing but a shell of himself. Not when he was so thin, the whites of his eyes starting to cloud. Not when he was sleeping more and more, and that cough made his lungs sound like rice paper in the rain, soaked and ready to split.

While she swirled away to tend to other customers, he stared down at his pie, but what would have once appealed to him now looked like a congealed, cloying mess. He couldn't eat. He couldn't even *think*.

He could only stare, frozen with indecision, and wonder if his choice would make a difference—or if Grey was too far gone.

Will he be angry with me, for choosing? For taking his choice away?

Will he be angry with me for even asking?

We made a deal. I just . . . never thought this would . . . I thought I could do this.

And I didn't expect to be so wrong.

He tore from his trance as Guineveve whisked back into his line of sight, her towel swiping across the counter.

"I might not be here the next time you come in," she said.

His head jerked up. "What? Why? I need to ask you—"

The shake of her head stalled him. "Everything? Aye, like as not. But I need to move on," she murmured regretfully. "You've survived dipping in and out of the world. I can't do it. It's too lonely. So instead of disappearing, instead of being alone . . . I just move elsewhere."

"You can leave?" His brows knit. "The longest I've been able to stay away from Savannah was two weeks in China in the nineties.

I nearly had to be hospitalized, and didn't know how to tell the doctors I wasn't ground zero for some new disease vector."

She snorted. "That's what you get for traveling overseas the same decade they released *Outbreak*." The rag twisted between her fingers. Her brows knit. "Aye, I can leave, but at a cost. You've really not the slightest clue about yourself, eh?"

"I'm like a baby with a slightly more advanced vocabulary."

"Compared to some of us, you *are* a wee babe. Haven't even broken four digits yet." She made an amused sound. "You've bound yourself to this place without even meaning to. Tied your life force up in the land and the people. Takes the place of what we lose, when we lose our connection to home. Helps keep us going a bit longer without needing to take a life. You trade freedom for a lower body count." She looked away, sighing, her eyes dark and her smile pained. "Thought about settling down somewhere myself. Putting down roots, as it were. I hear Ireland's nice this time of year."

"Is that home?" He leaned closer. "Is . . . that where we're from?"

"No. But the gateway to home may be there, if you believe the legends. If you believe we were never born human." She propped her chin in one hand. "I try not to worry about it. Home isn't home anymore. Tír na nÓg had no use for me, so I have no use for it."

"Tír na nÓg." He tried the word on, felt how it fit, like he'd said it a thousand times before but forgotten how. "I guess . . . I just want to know . . ."

"Why no one ever looked for you?"

"Sea," he offered, and smiled.

Her own smile faded. Her eyes clouded, and something he couldn't read flickered in them before she looked down, fingers knotting in her dishrag. "What makes you think they didn't?"

He ached, and started to reach for her. "Guineveve . . ."

"It doesn't matter," she said, a little too sharply—and pulled back, leaving him feeling lost, abandoned all over again. She smoothed her hands over her apron, then flashed a forced smile as overly bright as her glimmering eyes. "You'll be late for work, a leanbh."

A leanbh. My child.

Saint didn't know how he knew that, but he *knew*.

Reluctantly, he slid off his stool. This felt strangely like grieving, and he didn't understand why. "I'll come tomorrow to say goodbye."

"One thing you should learn, a leanbh." She sighed. "Never say goodbye if you don't have to."

✲⬧ 41 ⬦✲

He knew her now.

Grey painted the last crease in the full blossoms of blue-tinged lips, reflecting the same light as the charms in her hair, the rings on her fingers, the curls lying against her cheeks.

He knew her, and she seemed to look back at him past the coy curve of her lashes, and ask:

Grey Jean-Marcelin, what are you doing?

Is this how you use the gifts I give you?

He set the palette down and picked up a damp cloth to wipe his shaking fingers as he heard the creak of the elevator rolling up. By the time Saint stepped inside, already shrugging out of his jacket, Grey had managed to get his hands clean enough to risk settling them on Saint's hips and drawing him close.

"Hey. How was work?"

"Not as bad as usual. A couple of fender benders with whiplash, one idiot who fell off a frat house balcony."

Saint leaned in and kissed him lightly, but Grey felt it: that careful withdrawal again. The words Saint still wasn't telling him. He told himself to ask, but his mouth didn't want to open and the question sank like a rock inside him. He held his tongue as Saint crossed the room to look at his work for the night. If he were himself, if his body hadn't felt like a capsized ship, he would pin Saint to the wall and take him. Let him feel Grey's hunger.

But he didn't even have the energy left for that anymore, no matter how much he missed the sweetness of Saint's body and the way his voice rose high to the rafters.

He was close, he knew.

So why didn't he feel the peace he so desperately wanted?

He rested against Saint's shoulder while the other man looked over the new painting. His eyes softened, and he reached out to gently trace the driest edge of the canvas.

"Who is she?"

"Erzulie," Grey murmured. "Though there's a bit of an old university friend in her too . . . but in all her love and passion, she is my Erzulie."

"She's beautiful." Saint smiled faintly. "She's the first thing you've painted that isn't dead."

Grey started to speak—but choked off in a racking cough, a thick and phlegmy thing in his throat. It wouldn't *stop*, bowing him over until the pain broke his body in half, and Saint's voice was just a concerned haze past the noise of his own lungs tearing themselves apart. He didn't know what Saint was saying, but Grey felt his hands on him, helping him to bed, laying him down. Gentle touches, smoothing his brow, wiping his mouth. Covers laid over him. Something warm and honeyed tilted to his lips. Tea.

It's coming, he thought, looking up at the swimming blur of Saint's pale face. *It's coming. Erzulie, hold my hand until Bawon Samedi holds my heart.*

Saint sat against the headboard and leaned into him, his warmth leaching some of the coldness from Grey's flesh. He rested his head in Saint's lap as the coughs subsided, closing his eyes and counting his breaths until they steadied again.

Saint stroked his fingers over Grey's scalp, traced the upper curve of his ear, caressed the dash of his bullet scar where hair would never grow again. "Will you do something for me?"

"Hm?"

"Hold on." Saint made a hitched sound. "Hold on for a little longer."

He tilted his head back, looking up at Saint's profile from below with a faint smile. "I don't think that's in my control, Saint."

"No. But . . ." A shaky breath. "But it's in mine."

"What?"

"I can stop it."

"*What?*"

Betrayal wasn't a knife; it was a crushing iron fist, slamming into him and collapsing his rib cage. He pushed himself up, struggling on weakened arms, glaring at Saint.

"Why tell me this now?"

"Because I don't want you to die." Liquid eyes pleaded. "I don't think *you* want to die. I think you just . . . can't see any other way out."

"Don't. Don't tell me what I think or what I want, and don't you dare try to fix me."

"That's not what I'm trying to do." Saint wet his lips. "But I can be here for you while you look for another way yourself. That's what people do, isn't it? Building a . . . they call it a support structure, right? Someone to lean on."

"Who would I lean on if I *live*?" Panic threatened to break him. How could he be so close, only for Saint to get cold feet now? "You'll be dead. I'll be *alone*. You can't do that to me."

"That's . . ." Saint's eyes widened; he sucked in an audible breath. "You don't want to be alone anymore, do you? Because you lost your family, because . . ."

"Because nothing. Now you want me to live, and lose you? I can't. I won't!"

"But I can—"

"We agreed on this, Saint." A cough tried to crawl up his throat. He forced it back, swallowing the claws of it, heaving for breath and pressing his hand to his mouth. "We *agreed*!"

"I know." Saint's hands knotted in his lap. Those fucking white-bird hands that Grey had fixated on from the first moment, so expressive, so slender, and now they spoke volumes for pain, earnest entreaty, raw honest emotion. "But I hadn't realized when we agreed that I . . . I'd love you so easily. Enough to become human for you."

Grey stared. His bitterness, his frustration, arrested, caught in the grip of surprise. Saint . . . loved him? And yet the wild mad throbbing of his heart, the joy of it, the elation, the breathless sweetness, were dimmed—hidden beneath the bitter tang of confusion. Of having his certain path diverging again, splitting into two, five, ten, a dozen . . .

. . . and realizing he was no longer so sure which one he wanted to take.

"I don't understand," he said numbly.

"I can . . . I can take your place." Saint wrung his hands together. "Someone else could too, but if they were human it would just start the cycle over again. But if I willingly take your place, you won't die. And it strips me of my immortality. I won't die. I just . . . become human. That's all. I'll age and fade just like anyone else. A normal life. A normal life span."

And suddenly Grey saw it: a normal life, each day growing a little more wrinkled, a little more wise, a little more gray—and one of those divergent paths took him down a road where he saw crow's-feet etch around Saint's eyes and his hands spot with age, his skin thinning and softening and yet his grip still as perfect as it had for decades.

Something like that . . . something like that was never meant for him. Not when what he imagined could never be real. Not when the reality was filled with terrible holes of emptiness that could swallow him for days or months at a time, cutting pieces out of any relationship to leave it in tatters, turning every bond he formed self-destructive until he lost people the same way he'd lost Aminata.

And yet he *wanted* it.

But wanting it, making that choice for Saint, was the worst mistake he could possibly make.

He shook his head, ignoring his wavering vision. "Why didn't you tell me this before?"

"I didn't know." Saint's eyes brimmed, beads gathering on his lashes like rainfall. "That woman in the coffee shop. She's like me. She told me, just a few days ago."

"I . . ." Grey tried to reach for an answer. An emotion, but nothing was there. Like the overload had shorted him out, leaving nothing. Emptiness—and that emptiness was almost preferable, when it was familiar and safe. "I need time to think."

"But will you consider it?" Saint looked at him with a heartbreaking mixture of hope and despair, and he wanted to feel something, but he just . . . couldn't.

"Go home, Saint," he said.

And turned his face away, closing his eyes so he wouldn't have to watch him walk away.

✳⋵ 42 ⋶✳

He didn't know how long he stayed there after Saint left: numb, alone, feeling the emptiness in the apartment like a stain on his heart. His fault. Because Saint had offered him a gift more pure than even the gift of death, and Grey had shut down and rejected it. Shut down and withdrawn inside himself, to where he didn't have to weather the storm of the conflict inside him, safe in the eye of the hurricane.

That was what the numbness so often was.

Safe shelter for himself, even if it so easily demolished everything around him.

Across the room, Erzulie watched him with her limpid eyes. He could almost hear her voice in his head, that question. Her scorn for squandering her gifts.

He couldn't stand it.

He knew he shouldn't be trying to stand, trying to move, not when his legs were brittle sticks and his lungs were paper bellows, but he needed *air*, the noise of cars rushing past, the raucous cacophony of a city at night. He stood, wheezing, and struggled into his clothing, his shoes, before taking the elevator down and spilling out into the blistering night. His truck, he ignored. He didn't mean to go far. He just needed a walk, to stretch his limbs and feel his body one last time, to remember what it had been like before he was at death's door, to ask himself if he wanted that again.

How could he let Saint do that for him? How could he let Saint give up forever, when Saint was so very afraid of dying and Grey was so very afraid of living?

He stopped, looking up at the blurred halo of the streetlamps—and beyond that, the scatter of tiny stars, these great things made so small when seen from this trivial blue ball.

"That's what it's about, isn't it, Erzulie?" He sighed. "I'm afraid of living. I'm afraid of the pain of everyday things. I'm . . . I'm afraid of the dark that comes to every day, because one night the pain will blind me and I'll never be able to see the sun again."

That was the *why* of it that he'd never quite been able to articulate to Saint. Labeling it *depression* packaged it easily, but it was really that dread. That fear. That fear *of* fear, of being terrified that the next time he fell low, he'd lose the ability to climb back up.

"Tell me what to do," he pleaded—with the stars, with Erzulie, with the great dark hand that even now reached for him, asking so sweetly that he follow. "*Tell me.*"

But there was no answer. The loa would let him make his own path, even if it led him to ruin.

His phone weighed heavy in his pocket. He slipped it out, cradled it in his palm. He should call Saint. Tell him, *Come home, let's talk this out, we already know how it hurts when we try to do this alone.*

But as he scrolled through his contacts, he once more stopped on *A.* Her name. Her name, as fluid and soft as the curling spill of Erzulie's hair, painted in his brushstrokes.

And, his stomach rising up his throat, he tapped her contact and hit Call.

He almost didn't expect her to pick up. He thought she'd see his number, feel that echo of familiarity even though she'd probably deleted his contact years ago. And when the line clicked he sucked in a breath, struggling to think of what he'd say to her voice mail, until her warm, living voice came through:

"Hello?"

Grey's chest bottomed out. His lips moved uselessly, then formed her name. "Aminata?"

"*Grey?*" Shock clear in her voice, and he couldn't help but laugh, dry and tired.

"Yeah. It's me, Ami. It's me."

"Are you all right? I saw in the newspaper—"

He winced, and shifted to lean against a light post. "I lived through it. That's not why I'm calling."

Silence spoke: in hesitation, in doubt, in mistrust. Then she asked, her accent slow and careful, "Why *are* you calling? It's been six years, Grey. You don't just decide to call out of nowhere to ask how I've been."

"No? But I do want to know. How you've been. How . . . everything." He swallowed thickly. "I miss you in my life, Aminata. I miss my friend."

"That's what you called to tell me?"

He closed his eyes. ". . . No."

"Then what?"

"I . . . I called to say goodbye."

"What? Grey, what are you—"

"Let me finish."

If he even knew how. He thought he knew what he'd called to say, but all it took was the sound of her voice to shake that to pieces and leave him floundering. Aching. Filling up inside with something burning and scared, something fragile and trembling, something that remembered the warmth of her friendship and the rightness of having her in his life. Of having Saint in his life. Of letting himself be weak enough not to let go, but to *need*, and to trust that if he asked them to catch him, they would.

"I called to say goodbye," he said. His eyes were wet, the street turning into a mass of twisting colors. "But I can't. I can't say goodbye to you, to him—"

"To who?"

"*Let me finish.*" He had to get it out all at once, or he wouldn't at all. "I'm sorry. That's what I really called to say. I'm sorry that I pushed you away. I'm sorry that I let you go. I'm sorry that I couldn't admit that I needed help. I *need* help. I wasn't coping with my depression then, and I'm not coping much better now. But it was easier to think I was sparing you by letting you go than it was to admit to you that I'm this broken."

He didn't know what he expected her to say. But it wasn't the soft, sympathetic sound she made, before murmuring, "You're not broken, Grey."

"No?"

"No more than anyone else. I've always known you hid your little hurts . . . but I wish you'd told me. I wish you hadn't shut me out."

"I know. And I know it wasn't fair to make you try so much, only to push you away. But I'm not pushing now. I'm telling you now. I'm telling you the truth."

"Why?"

"Because I want you back in my life. I want my friend back. I want to see you."

"You want a lot."

"Only if it's what you want, too."

"What I want is gone. Who we were before is gone. That's just a memory. We're different people now. I don't even know what you *look* like anymore." She crushed him with every word, until she continued, "But that doesn't mean we can't try something new."

He felt like a fool that he had to sniffle before he could speak, rubbing at his nose, grinning broad and stupid. "Yeah?"

"Yeah. But are you gonna be here for it this time, Grey?"

That was one hell of a question. One he'd been asking himself for far too long. One that had spat from the mouth of the shotgun as he'd pulled the trigger.

He looked down at his spidered, emaciated hand through the blur of tears. It wasn't the hand of a dead man; just the hand of a dying one, but that could change if he reached out and took what Saint offered, grasped it in his fingers and cherished it close.

If he decided to be here for this, in all its pain and pitfalls.

If he could trust people to be here for *him*, and not hate himself for every moment of need.

"Yeah," he said, and felt a weighty rightness settle inside him with the single word. "Yeah. I'll be here for it."

"I'm gonna hold you to that. Idiot." Her sniffle came loud over the phone. "Now stop fucking crying. You're fucking up my contact lenses."

He laughed. "No more glasses?"

"You've missed a lot. I'm *chic* now. And these things itch when they get crusty." She laughed, her voice thick over the line, a little clotted in a way he understood too well. "I've gotta go. My daughter's quiet, which means she's plotting the downfall of Western civilization."

His breaths caught. "You have a daughter?"

"Yeah. She's three. Her name's Idrissa. You want to meet her? She's a little demon."

"Like mother, like daughter." Bondye, Aminata had a *daughter*. While he'd been stuck in one place, life had moved on around him, and he wondered at all the small little joys he'd missed. "Coffee? Bring the kid. I'll watch my tongue."

"You'll teach her how to swear in Kreyole, you mean." She chuckled. "But yeah. Coffee sounds good. Call me this weekend. We'll set a date."

"I'd like that."

"And Grey?"

"Yeah?"

"If you ever take this long to call me again, *I will end you.*"

He laughed, almost dizzy with it. He felt light, too light, as if he were lifting out of his body, high as when the fire took him and burning with something strange and terrifying. "Love you too, Ami," he said, and realized he meant it.

Realized he was giving himself permission to love again.

He ended the call and slumped against the light post, scrubbing at his cheeks. Fuck. What was he *doing*? He didn't even know. Not anymore. But he suddenly *wanted*: wanted to know all the small things that had passed him by, wanted to try, wanted to know if loving Saint was anything other than doomed.

He just . . . *wanted*, period, when for the longest time he'd wanted nothing than for everything to end.

His chest ached. He should go back, go to bed, sleep until he was strong enough to talk to Saint again, to sort this out, to choose. He turned down the sidewalk, reversing his path, but his legs buckled. He gasped, clutched at the light post, forced himself up even though his body tried to crumple and collapse, tried to dump him onto the pavement. Just a few blocks home. A few blocks to his bed, and he could rest. Those small things would still be there tomorrow, when he had the life left to face them.

He struggled a few more cold-sweating steps, his tongue a cottony slug inside his mouth, his eyes aching as he fought them to focus. Then the strings holding him up unraveled, and this time there was no light post to catch him, nothing to stop him from spilling to the sidewalk and tumbling into the street, grit scraping against his skin as he tried to catch himself and failed, burns raking acid along his hands and arms. He heard screams. Honks. The screech of tires. The snarl of an engine.

Then pain, crunching ragged teeth into him in bloody squirts, piercing his body and filling his world with red.

This was familiar, he thought, as crimson filled his vision and turned the sky violet. He was dimly aware of people moving around him, but everything came down a dark tunnel as he retreated from the pain, into a shadowed gloom that folded over him like a cloak.

"Grey?"

That beloved voice. He forced his eyes open and looked through that distant tunnel at Saint's face—his wide, tear-filled eyes, Grey's blood on his hands, his lips parted and saying frantic things he couldn't make out.

Saint, he tried to say, but the name wouldn't come. He tried to reach for his hand, but he was too weak. Too far gone.

I can't die like this, he thought, even as he realized he'd come full circle, their relationship ending as it had begun. *I can't die without seeing him again.*

✳❧ 43 ☙✳

Multiple compound fractures.

Concussion with intracranial swelling. Possible internal hemorrhaging. Those were the words on Grey's chart, and Saint hated them. He fucking hated them. He hated how clinical they were, how they packaged up the broken man in the hospital bed and turned him into a neatly discarded bundle of tidy medical conditions.

Those words didn't encompass the shock of spilling out of the ambulance to see Grey lying in the street while the ambulance flashed its lights and red strobed hellish illumination over the accident scene. The heartbreak of that strange smile on his lips as his eyes faded and went blank. The terror of feeling his heart stop under Saint's palm, only to frantically force him back to life with compressions and paddles and sheer, desperate willpower, even as he wondered if Grey would hate Saint for bringing him back.

Or the despair of sitting here for days on end with Grey's limp fingers clasped in his own, waiting while Grey's breaths fogged the tubes inserted into his nostrils.

Waiting, and begging him to wake.

"Did you do this on purpose?" he whispered. He talked to Grey nearly every day, but there was never any response. Doctors hesitated to describe Grey's condition as comatose, but if he wasn't, then he was standing on the edge of that fucking cliff—and Saint held tight to his hand, as if he could keep him from falling over into the dark. "Grey. Please. Not like this." His eyes were gritty with the tears he'd cried, his throat burning. "Wake up for me. Please."

Nothing.

Saint bowed his head, a keen of misery rising up his throat as he pressed his brow to Grey's shoulder. It felt like mourning, but he wouldn't let it be. He refused to grieve as if Grey were already dead. Not when he needed to see him again so badly. Just once, if Grey wanted to die this much. Just one more time so he could apologize for pushing him, for taking back their vow.

He didn't know how he'd let go, but he'd try.

But he didn't think he could stand this eternity without Grey.

"Please," he whispered again, but he didn't know who he was pleading with. Maybe Grey's loa, if they were listening. If the Erzulie he loved so much still loved him. "I know I don't have the right to want him to live, but I . . ."

He whimpered, his heart a tiny knot, a heavy stone, a wrinkled thing struggling to beat when he felt like the blood of his life had spilled all over the ground while Grey had bled out beneath him.

". . . I can't stand to see him die."

✳ 44 ✳

For the second time in his life, Grey Jean-Marcelin came back from the dead.

He woke in more pain than he could remember in his life. The last time had just been one scorching line down his throbbing skull, but this . . . this was a living beast crouched on his chest and slowly digging its claws between his ribs, into his skull, into the pit of his stomach, even sticking two up his nose. He groaned, tried to shift, tried to throw the beast off, but it only dug in harder until its snarl was a scream echoing through his entire body.

"Well," he said, mumbling around a bloated tongue, a desert-dry mouth, an itching throat. "That hurts."

Something clutched against his hand. Some*one*. He didn't have to open his eyes to know who, when he knew that touch better than he knew his own, knew that warm, soft hand as if it were etched in his DNA.

"Grey," Saint breathed. "Grey, you're *awake*."

He forced his eyes to open: gritty, rusty things on scratchy hinges. The hospital. A room so identical it might as well have been the same as before. But he didn't care about the room, didn't care about the tubes up his nose or the casts on his limbs or the IV needle in his arm. Didn't care about that terrible medicinal smell or the steady beep of the heart monitor or what he was pretty sure was a catheter in his fucking *dick*. The last thing he'd seen before the darkness claimed him had been Saint's face wet with tears—and that same lovely face shone with the tracks of spilling wetness as Saint leaned over him, sniffling, his lips swollen and his cheeks blotchy and his nose red and his eyes rimmed scarlet around the edges.

He'd never seen anything more beautiful in his life.

His lips felt wooden, but he forced a smile, mouth cracking, aching. "Saint. Hi."

"You idiot." Saint's voice broke on a sob; he pressed a hand over his mouth. "Why did you—"

"I didn't." His throat didn't want to work, itching and croaking, but he forced it when he needed Saint to know. To understand. He hadn't tried to kill himself. "I swear it was an accident. I went for a walk and got dizzy and fell into traffic."

"You've been . . . I . . ." Saint trailed off, his lips trembling, and shook his head.

"How long was I out?"

"Six days. You had . . . you had intracranial swelling. They had to put a shunt in to drain the fluid. The doctor was afraid even if you survived, it would be with brain damage."

He smiled faintly. "Wasn't much there to damage."

"This isn't funny!" Saint flared, sniffling, gulping back a raw sound.

"I know. I know it's not. I'm sorry." He tried to squeeze his hand and just barely managed to twitch his fingers. He felt like everything on the path between his brain and fingertips was broken. "You stayed with me."

"You think I wouldn't?"

"I'm glad you did. Just . . ." He wet his lips, then made a grateful sound as Saint dipped a bit of gauze in a cup of water and dabbed over his mouth before carefully tipping in a blessed sip of coolness that bloomed on his tongue, loosened his voice, dredged up the words he'd needed to say since before he was stupid enough to fall into fucking traffic. "I went for a walk to think. To choose. And that choice was almost taken away from me. But I'm scared, Saint."

"Of what?"

"Of living." Maybe now wasn't the best time to say this, but it was fresh and raw in his mind, the last thing before those headlights had come bearing down on him, the first thing when his mind had pieced itself back together. "Of trying again—because I feel like I could, right now. But that feeling won't last, and I'll be back down into the dark again. Alone."

"Not alone." Saint leaned over him, clutching his hand so tight it hurt, but the pain was worth it. "I can't pull you out of the dark. But I can stay there with you."

"What if I'm not worth it? What if you give up hundreds of years for me . . . and I'm not worth it?"

"You thought I was worth dying for, when I didn't."

"That's different."

"How?" Saint asked, rushed, fervent. "One thing I've learned in two hundred years is that part of life is being afraid of the bad times. It's worse when you can't even control how you feel about it, because you can't control the things inside your mind. I can't know how that feels. Not completely." His gaze darted away, then back. Nervous, earnest . . . sweet, brimming with emotion as he met Grey's eyes, burning with the things he normally guarded as if he could protect both Grey and himself from the pressure of *need*. "But I can care. I can be here to make it less frightening to try again, Grey." His mouth worked, then softened into a sigh. "But I won't ask you to choose that for me."

"If not for you . . . then why?"

"For you." Saint touched his cheek—and Grey realized there was a bandage there when soft fingertips feathered along its edges, tracing him as if relearning his broken and rearranged pieces. "You said the world you left behind would be empty and colorless . . . but you're what gives it color. You're so fucking beautiful. If there's anything left in you that you still love . . ."

The pain of crushed flesh was nothing to the pain of asking himself that question, and not knowing the answer. Of reaching for an answer, thinking that maybe that spark of wanting inside him would fill that void, that it would be so easy . . . and yet there was still that same nothingness, without explanation and without answer.

But maybe he was never meant to know. Maybe that was what it meant to be alive.

Not knowing, but always, always searching.

"Maybe," he said, and Saint offered a wavering smile full of hope.

"A maybe isn't a no."

"A maybe is a tomorrow. And one more tomorrow is better than none." He wanted so much to reach for Saint, but he couldn't move. "You want to be human for me?"

"I want to be human for both of us."

"I . . ."

Say it. Say it, do it, fuck, be brave. Be brave. You were brave with Ami. You can be brave with Saint. You used to know how. You used to be able to lift yourself up. And maybe he couldn't anymore, but maybe . . .

"I want to try," he said. "Therapy again, or . . . something. But I can't make any promises."

"Don't make promises. Promises break too easily."

"Easier than immortal curses?"

With a choked laugh, Saint leaned down, leaned over him, rested his brow to Grey's—until Grey could see nothing but sunset eyes and pale skin and the fall of dark hair, smell nothing but burned caramel and green apples, feel nothing but the warmth of his breath and the softness of his flesh, eclipsing the pain. "Just wake up with me tomorrow and the day after, Grey. And the day after that, and the day after that. Can you be happy with that?"

"I can. I will." Even if it caused him pain, even if it shot up his arm in radiating tremors, he lifted his hand and slipped trembling fingers into that dark, tangled hair. "Just . . . be with me when I'm at my darkest, Saint. And I'll try."

"Always."

He smiled, and for once . . . for once it didn't feel like lying to himself. "Kiss me?" he asked, and Saint laughed, brittle around a fresh flood of tears.

"Are you sure you can handle it?"

"*Please.*"

More than anything, he wanted to draw that sweet mouth to his—but Saint came to him. Soft at first, barely a breath of touch, just enough to make longing explode inside him with the need for more, the need for this to be *real*, to remind himself that he was alive and terrified and yet for some insane reason, he wanted to try again.

Loving Saint couldn't fix him. Maybe nothing could fix him. But kissing him like this, with the taste of his tears caught between them and the tang of salt only heightening the honeyed sweetness of his warmth, his depths, every loving taste . . .

It made him feel like he didn't need to be fixed, as long as he managed to survive.

He leaned up toward Saint, straining into him, *needing* him—only to hiss as his ribs became knives, and forced him back down with his vision swimming and his skull on fire.

". . . Ow."

"Stupid," Saint teased.

"Yeah. I am." He chuckled, then winced and closed his eyes against a dizzy, reeling tilt of vertigo that made the ceiling arc past. "But I think it's time I gave myself permission to be."

"To be stupid?"

"To be flawed." He opened his eyes, looking up at his Saint. His leanan sidhe. His loa, his angel . . . but so much more. "To be human."

"Yeah?"

Saint smiled, and in that smile was something Grey had never thought either of them could ever know: a chance to start over. And maybe this was still a fever dream, maybe this was madness, maybe he was broken . . . but he wanted to *try.*

And that, for him, was no small thing.

"I'm starting to think," Saint said, "human doesn't sound like a half-bad thing to be. I'm ready, Grey."

His eyes widened. He reached for Saint's hand, fumbling blindly until their fingers laced. "Now? You don't need more time to think? I don't want to rush you, it doesn't have to be—"

"It does." A steady hand, a steady gaze held his. "There's not much left in you, Grey. I barely pulled you back. It needs to be now. I *want* it to be now. Two hundred years is long enough to think." Saint's eyes softened. "I don't want you to doubt me. So let me do it now."

"I never doubted you, love."

Saint smiled wistfully. "Maybe I doubted myself."

Grey lingered on that smile, as he traced his thumb over Saint's knuckles. Was he worthy, for a spirit to make himself human for his sake? Could he stand the pressure of trying to be?

Until he realized, as he met Saint's eyes . . . that Saint would never ask him to.

"How does it work?" he asked. "Is there some kind of ritual, or—"

Saint laughed, a sound so sweet that for a moment Grey could see him as he once might have been: fey and wild and not of this world, elfin and beautifully timeless and strange. "Grey? Shut up and let it just *be*."

Before Grey could say another word, Saint leaned down and kissed him. Dark hair fell around them both in a cool curtain, shutting out the world—and Grey took the pain, took the ache in his bones, took whatever punishment he had to, to press into that kiss. This, in this moment, was everything he could ever want. Everything he could ever need. And as the taste of Saint stole into him, honeyed and otherworldly and delicate as dew, he sighed out his name and drew in an answering sigh on his next breath.

And yet with that breath came something else: a torrent, bursting and hot, a blazing rush as if he'd touched the sun. The fire. The fire that had driven him to paint, that had burned him apart from the inside out to leave only a hollow shell filled with the clinging ashes of a soul. It burned him, consumed him, eclipsed him, and he cried out against lips that tasted of that molten gold burn and everything he had spilled from himself and onto canvases painted in his heart's blood.

Saint's kiss gentled, as if he could ease the onslaught, soothe the pain. Grey gasped against his mouth as the blaze consolidated into a single livid burning point, centered on his shoulder. His skin felt like acid, etched in and searing deep, and he bit back a cry.

Slowly, Saint's lips parted from his. Slowly, Grey opened his eyes. For a moment he could see nothing, the room a white haze, before he blinked it away and Saint's face came clear, hovering over him and watching him with concern. He looked . . . different, Grey realized dazedly, though he couldn't quite put his finger on it. A trace of that near-artificial perfection and beauty chipped away to leave a certain unpolished roughness: the slight crook of his nose a touch more pronounced, his worried smile a little lopsided, his skin no longer so flawlessly smooth.

He looked more *real*, Grey realized, and thought he'd never seen Saint look more lovely.

"Are you all right?" Saint asked hoarsely, and cupped a palm to Grey's cheek, pale fingers shaking, soft skin cooler than Grey remembered and yet so much more human, without the blazing heat of stolen lives captured in Saint's flesh. When Grey turned his head to nuzzle into Saint's fingers, it no longer hurt to move. Breathing no longer felt like straining air through punctured lungs. He still *hurt*, his bruises and broken bones screaming, but it was the loud, angry cry of a body in revolt and not the whisper of a last dying breath.

He was whole again, he realized, and the timer had been set back.

While for Saint, it had only just begun to count down.

Closing his eyes, he lifted Saint's fingers to his lips, kissed them, pressed his mouth to each fingertip one by one. He had no words to answer how he felt, that Saint had made this choice—for him, with him. And so he only held his touch close, and hoped he would be able to for many years to come.

"I . . ." Grey shook his head. "What about you? Are you all right?"

"Cold." Saint's laugh sounded almost incredulous. "It's so hot out the blacktop is melting, and I'm *cold*. This place is a freezer."

Grey nuzzled Saint's palm. "Is it too much to bear?"

"No—no, it's not. But . . . Grey."

A touch to Grey's arm prompted him to open his eyes. Saint had pulled the blankets down and tugged the sleeve of his hospital gown up over his biceps, baring skin that still felt too *tight*, as if Grey were filled to overflowing with a life too large for this mortal shell.

"Look," Saint said.

Grey craned to look as much as he could when three-quarters of his body was immobilized, strapped down. Where that burn had touched his arm, fresh lines of shimmer-dark ink glowed on his skin, etched deep against dark brown. An owl perched on his shoulder with its wings spread, curving over the arch of muscle with feathers gracefully and delicately flexed, its strange eyes watchful and knowing. A tattoo. Just like Saint's, branded into his flesh, and he understood now:

The tattoo *was* Saint. Saint's life on his skin, just as his life had been drawn into Saint's flesh in the spreading spires of pointed antlers. He let out a soft, wondering breath.

"How did you *do* that?"

"I just . . . let go." Saint shrugged, wry and self-deprecating. "I think it's time to let a lot of things go."

"But not me, I hope."

"No. Not you," Saint swore, and in those words was the fear that Grey lived every day. The fear of making the wrong choice, of being alone, of facing life at all. Yet it was a fear they could share, a weight that couldn't crush them as long as they carried it between them. "I'll never let go of you."

"Saint." His heart swelled. Somehow they had come full circle. Somehow Saint had given him back his life—but where once it had been a curse, now it was a promise. He searched for the right thing to say, but there was only one thing. The only thing that could ever truly matter. "Saint, I love you."

Saint laughed, swaying closer. "So you've made clear."

"I don't even get to hear it back?"

"Mm . . . I need to do one more thing."

"What?"

"This."

While Grey watched, he fished a digital recorder from his pocket. An impish smile curved his lips as he lifted it to his mouth and pressed the button.

"My name is Saint," he said, his clear, quiet voice lilting over the hospital room, that accent like music, like prayer—until Grey forgot the sterile medicinal smell, forgot the shadow of death, forgot everything except the bond writ between them in ink, in blood, in loss, in hope, in words more perfect than any he'd heard in his life. "And I'm in love with Grey Jean-Marcelin."

A WORD FROM
THE AUTHOR

We all know love can't cure depression. Sometimes the strongest support network in the world can't fill the emptiness, bring the color back into the world, find those reservoirs of lost energy, silence the harmful, sometimes outright dangerous thoughts. I avoided wandering down that path with this story—avoided a tale of some magical cure-all, a panacea where love somehow erases the reality of depression and someone else is able to fix Grey in a way that he couldn't fix himself.

That's not realistic. That's not a healthy expectation to put on yourself or anyone else. That's not true, and perpetuating that idea is damaging to people who live with depression every day. People who struggle enough to fight for themselves, without being told the only way they'll ever be whole is through the unpredictable, entirely fraught, and sometimes wonderful, sometimes terrible tangle of falling in love. Particularly for Black and non-Black people of color, for whom mental health and access to mental health care are heavy issues that are so often ignored as part of the systemic and structural problems we deal with every day.

There's no real "fix" for depression. Not in another person, not in a bottle. There are coping methods. Medications. Therapeutic treatments that vary from person to person. Nothing is perfect, but the important thing I wanted you to take away from this story is that you don't have to be. Perfect, that is. And if sometimes you need to just lie down and let things be too much for you for a day or two, if you need to tap out for a mental health day, if sometimes the meds don't work and the therapist just makes it worse and you don't know what to do . . .

That's okay.

And it's okay to be tired of everyone trying to fix you, instead of accepting you and loving you while you do what you need to live with yourself in the way that makes you happy.

But it's just as okay to need a hand up, a support network, to remind you to keep trying on those days when you *want* to get up and yet can't get your legs beneath you.

Because depression sucks. I should know. I have it. It's pushed me to some scary extremes in the past. And it will tell you for days or months or years at a time that you can't cope. It'll reiterate every horrid thing you've thought about yourself until you believe them, and think everyone around you believes them, too. It will make you lie down and give up, and at the time you'll almost willingly buy into those thoughts because they feel like yours instead of the thoughts of some parasite inside you, sucking the will to just *be* out of your brain.

It's only when you get a chance to come up for air that you realize those thoughts weren't you, but even then there's doubt. Wondering. Wondering if the depressive you is the real you, or if the upswing you is the real you, or if the medicated you is the real you, or . . .

The real you is the one who makes it through day to day. Whether you're depressive or dreamy, whether you're down or dancing in the streets. You're going to change day to day. What you believed with utter conviction one day you'll let go of the next, just like Grey letting go of his conviction that he needed to die even while embracing his complete and utter fear to live. And the thing is, that's okay. It's okay to change, to spin, to divert course, to double back. Finding your way isn't as simple as Point A to Point B, and you're going to find yourself course-correcting a lot as you try to work out what's right for you and what isn't. Sometimes it's something you need to do alone. Sometimes you need someone to give you a hand. It may be someone who loves you. It may be a stranger.

But it's okay to reach out and say, "Hey. I'm spinning. Hold me steady for just a minute, until I can stop myself."

And if you don't want to turn to the people in your life, that doesn't mean you have no one reaching for you. Because there are people waiting out there to talk to you. People who *want* to. Who will hold your hand in the dark, without making you come out until you're good and ready. And you can find some of those people right here:

The National Depression Hotline: crisistextline.org

The National Suicide Prevention Lifeline:
suicidepreventionlifeline.org

Hope for Depression's Treatment Resources by State:
hopefordepression.org/depression-facts/treatment-resources

And many, many more. There are resources out there. People to talk to, when you're ready.

Only when you're ready.

Until then, do whatever you need to do to be good to yourself.

Dear Reader,

Thank you for reading Xen Sanders's *Shatterproof*!

We know your time is precious and you have many, many entertainment options, so it means a lot that you've chosen to spend your time reading. We really hope you enjoyed it.

We'd be honored if you'd consider posting a review—good or bad—on sites like **Amazon, Barnes & Noble, Kobo, Goodreads, Twitter, Facebook, Tumblr,** and your blog or website. We'd also be honored if you told your friends and family about this book. Word of mouth is a book's lifeblood!

For more information on upcoming releases, author interviews, blog tours, contests, giveaways, and more, please sign up for our weekly, spam-free newsletter and visit us around the web:

Newsletter: tinyurl.com/RiptideSignup
Twitter: twitter.com/RiptideBooks
Facebook: facebook.com/RiptidePublishing
Goodreads: tinyurl.com/RiptideOnGoodreads
Tumblr: riptidepublishing.tumblr.com

Thank you so much for Reading the Rainbow!

RiptidePublishing.com

ACKNOWLEDGMENTS

So much love to Sarah Lyons for this opportunity—and for your patience, understanding, and kindness while we worked to find the best path for this book. Thank you to L.C. Chase for a gorgeous cover that reignited my writing fire and made me feel the breathless wonder of seeing one of my books represented in such a way. And thank you to Alex Whitehall, for such insightful copy edits and attention to detail that made sure this book was the best it could possibly be. I've enjoyed working with the Riptide staff, and appreciate more than I can say the time, effort, and faith that went into this project.

To my friends: you know you mean everything to me. Nic for reminding me every day why I do this, and listening to me incessantly nitpick every detail and ask "Does this ping wrong to you?" a million times over. Tarah for being *you*, with your sweetness and constant support, encouragement, and faith that I can do this (and so can you, in case you forgot). Sabrina, for writing with me every day so we can keep each other accountable, and for being there for the past ten years as we developed as writers and as friends. Amanda, for that dry wit and trademark cynicism that keep me in check; I actually have an "Amanda check" filter in my head for whether or not a story element or dialogue would make you give me that *look*. And Lyra, for always having a bright word to say and a kick in the butt even on the days when I say, "I don't know if I can do this." I'd never be here without any of you.

And to my friends on social media: we may never have met face-to-face, but your support, enthusiasm, and encouragement have been a large part of what makes this worth it—to know that on some level you aren't just connecting with my stories, but connecting with *me*, and feeling these stories that I carve out of myself to share with you.

Thank you, everyone. You're amazing.

I should close this with some kind of "wind beneath my wings" comment.

. . .

Nope.

ALSO BY
XEN SANDERS

Writing as Cole McCade
The Lost: A Crow City Novel (Crow City, #1)
The Fallen: A Crow City Prequel Novella (Crow City, #1.5)
A Second Chance at Paris (Bayou's End, #1)
Zero Day Exploit (Bayou's End, #1.5)
Sometimes It Storms (Part of the *Winter Rain* charity anthology)

ABOUT THE AUTHOR

Xen Sanders is a New Orleans-born Southern boy without the Southern accent, currently residing somewhere in the metropolitan wilds of the American Midwest. He spends his days as a suit-and-tie corporate consultant and business writer, and his nights writing genre-bending science fiction and fantasy tinged with a touch of horror and flavored by the influences of his multiethnic, multicultural, multilingual background—when he's not being tackled by two hyperactive cats. He wavers between calling himself bisexual and calling himself queer, but no matter what word he uses he's a staunch advocate of LGBTQIA representation and visibility in genre fiction.

He also writes contemporary romance and erotica as Cole McCade. And while he spends more time than is healthy hiding in his writing cave instead of hanging around social media, you can generally find him in these usual haunts:

Email: blackmagic@blackmagicblues.com
Twitter: @thisblackmagic
Facebook: facebook.com/xen.cole
Facebook Fan Page: facebook.com/ColeMcCadeBooks
Website & Blog: blackmagicblues.com
Dammit, Cole Advice Column:
    blackmagicblues.com/category/dammit-cole
The Speak Project: blackmagicblues.com/speak
Street Team / Fan Group:
    facebook.com/groups/mccadesmarauders

Enjoy more stories like
Shatterproof
at RiptidePublishing.com!

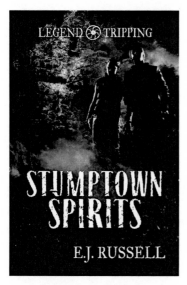

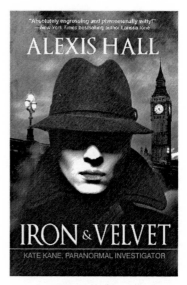

Stumptown Spirits
ISBN: 978-1-62649-409-1

Iron & Velvet
ISBN: 978-1-62649-049-9

Earn Bonus Bucks!

Earn 1 Bonus Buck for each dollar you spend. Find out how at
RiptidePublishing.com/news/bonus-bucks.

Win Free Ebooks for a Year!

Pre-order coming soon titles directly through our site and you'll
receive one entry into a drawing for a chance to win free books for
a year! Get the details at RiptidePublishing.com/contests.

CPSIA information can be obtained
at www.ICGtesting.com
Printed in the USA
LVOW12s2302171116
513494LV00001B/112/P